"A narrative rich in vivid portraits, ... realism, of unexplored Staten Island life."

—*Christina LaRocca*

"A new voice emerges from the forgotten borough in fiction beautifully painted across a historical backdrop."

—*Marc Pitanza*

SPEED MY WAY UP

SPEED MY WAY UP

Selected Stories

KRISTIN PITANZA

Full Court Press
Englewood Cliffs, New Jersey

Published in the United States of America
by Full Court Press, 601 Palisade Avenue,
Englewood Cliffs, NJ 07632
fullcourtpressnj.com

ISBN 978-1-946989-20-8
Library of Congress Catalog No. 2018957386

Editing by Barry Sheinkopf and Stephen Greeley

Book design by Barry Sheinkopf

Cover photograph by Gaspar Pitanza

Cover design by Yenory Ortiz Pitanza

Author photo by Lou Affortunato

This project is made possible (in part) by a DCA Premier
Grant from Staten Island Arts, with public funding from
the New York City Department of Cultural Affairs.

TO STATEN ISLAND AND ITS PEOPLE

Acknowledgements

Several individuals helped me make this project a reality. I want to thank them all. First, my parents, for inspiring me to follow my dreams. My father, Gaspar Pitanza, for letting me use his photograph. To my mother, Connie Pitanza, for inspiring me to write *Speed My Way Up*. Christopher Campbell, for telling me about the grid that detected promotions in the police department. April Cass Buono, for tolerating my persistence and dedication, for realizing my passion and helping me paint a picture. Barry Sheinkopf, for his patience, support, and assiduous critique of my pronoun use. Stephen Greeley, for meeting with me, making my stories better, and looking at my work conceptually. Clare Anastasiou, for cultural contributions and pointing out poor diction. Marc Pitanza, for inspiring me to be better. Lou Affortunato, for his unconditional love and insight. A special thanks to my sister-in-law, Yenory Ortiz Pitanza, for creating an amazing cover.

A special thanks to the Department of Cultural Affairs at Staten Island Arts for making this project possible. A portion of the proceeds of this venture will go to The Joyful Heart Foundation.

TABLE OF CONTENTS

SPEED MY WAY UP

BETH ANN AND DAN, BOTH in their early thirties, began their mornings in bed with a little whiskey in their coffee. On her nightstand, a yellow radio with a reclining Mickey Mouse on top—one of the newer collectibles items on the market—was tuned to a New York City soul station. Dan had brought home the radio for her a few weeks before, after one of his jobs, and every night since then, before she went to bed, she would rub its head for good luck.

That spring morning, the well-known DJ Frankie "Hollywood" Crocker, famed for playing his quiet storm songs, was airing William "Rosko" Mercer's "Peacemaker." Beth Ann began humming the music to herself as she closed her eyes and asked Dan whether or not the train toward the South Shore was running on the AM schedule.

He sweetly said, "No, baby, we'll wait till noon—no sense in going in the morning. Too congested."

Beth Ann had dark, smooth skin like her mother, who was only about twenty years older than she and worked as a cleaning and maintenance woman in the house they were renting a room in. Beth Ann—petite and dainty—was about five-four and very well kept. She had an angular, pointed nose and dark brown, almond-shaped eyes. Her lips were voluptuous and soft, with a naturally sexy pucker. She had dyed her hair an auburn brown that nicely complemented her dark skin.

Sipping her coffee, she began to feel a pull in her neck. She had wrapped her hair the night before and realized that maybe she had done it a little too tight. Dan saw the anxiousness in her face, reached for her neck, and began to rub it gently, murmuring, "You gots to be careful when you wrap your hair at night, baby. You look more beautiful with your hair natural anyways."

"I know. I know that's what you thinkin', but it don't look right when I wear it *natural*," she replied, mocking his sultry tone.

Dan was a stocky man a few inches taller than she was. He had a sweet face people trusted at first sight. His nose was flat; his dark eyes bulged and, being goofy and watery, brought to mind a puppy dog; yet part of his upper lip flopped over his lower one, like the lips of a fish. He had some dark moles and crevices on his upper cheekbones, and some that rode along the top of his brow. His hair was short, combed over to one side, and shaved on either side of his head with a single-edged razor, exposing very large, pointy ears.

He took a last sip of coffee, set the bone-colored porcelain cup down on a matching saucer on his nightstand, and began to stretch his muscular arms. He rubbed the back of Beth Ann's neck some more. She cooed, "Stop that!" and moved his hand away, laughing. He had known it would get a rise out of her.

He rose and began to do a little dance to "CHAKA-Chas" on the way to their dresser, where Beth Ann's musical jewelry box sat and where he had hidden a gift earlier that morning while she was asleep.

"I picked up a little something for you last week at my last job," he said, "and I wasn't sure when to give it to you." He lifted the lid of the music box sitting on top of a cheap dresser as he turned and looked at her. The gift was draped over a plastic ballerina with a mesh tutu. Light streaming through the stained-glass window above the dresser fell onto his face. "Here you go," he said as he held up a double string of pearls with an 18-karat gold clasp.

Her hands flew to her cheeks. She looked up at him and

gasped, "Those are *my* pearls?"

"Yes, my love, these are for you and only you!"

THEY HAD FINALLY GOTTEN to the afternoon train at the Clifton Station. They marched out the door of the two-floor colonial where they were renting a room. They hustled down the sycamore-lined streets that residents cared for and that, from a certain angle, looked like rows of bottle brushes.

She hurried to get to the train as quickly as possible, Dan following stealthily, as if plotting something. Her brown tweed palazzo pants got caught on a rose thorn protruding from a neighbor's home. The sleeveless shirt that came to her knees and that she wore with a black sheath turtleneck gave her a crisp, professional look. She always wore platforms because she was so petite, and the vinyl cuffs were pinching her feet. She and her mother had taken a trip to the Woolworth's in Stapleton a few nights before and bought a few things, including the damn shoes that she hadn't broken in yet.

That spring day the sun was shining brightly, but there was a nice cool breeze. She had wrapped a sheer white kerchief around her head, so the wind wouldn't mess her carefully sprayed and newly done do. She had it in a short, neat bob.

Dan tried to tug playfully at the handkerchief, then slip beside her as if he hadn't. She turned, annoyed and surprised, then turned back, and he laughed. She asked, "Do you think you're *funny*, Mr. Dan Smith?" She laughed too and pulled a piece of lint out of his hair. She had a natural doe tilt at the corner of her eyes. They crinkled when she looked annoyed or laughed, and just then she was annoyed. He gave her his big dopey look, trying not to giggle. They kissed and walked side by side to the crosswalk.

Dan's brown sport coat with suede patch elbows was making him hot. Beth Ann exclaimed, "Ya know, there are so many ways for you to look professional, there ain't no reason to be wearing something so heavy on a spring day."

They looked as polished as possible for the kinds of things they were going to do. The gold onyx ring that he wore on his middle finger glittered in the sun as he wrapped his arm around Beth Ann and said, "Dear, just let me be, and let me complain as I will."

At that instant they heard a panicked voice coming from behind them, "*Beth Ann, Beth Ann!*" It was her mother, Clarice, in her cleaning attire—a floral housecoat wrap, a pair of baby-blue scrub pants, and white clogs.

Startled, Beth turned. "What's wrong, Mama?"

Clarice, exasperated and out of breath, said, "I didn't know if I remembered to tell you that the man had a very deep accent. I think it was Eyetalian or something. He was laying tile for the McCoys when I heard him talkin'. If you meet the wife, she may not speak English. Heard him say he has two daughters. Don't forget—Justin Avenue, right under the railroad trestle."

Beth Ann rolled her eyes and looked at her reassuringly as Dan held her hand, rubbing her fingers. She said, "I know, Mama, you told us the other day. Now, get back to work before old man Manfredi sees you walking the streets—and you have to pick up the baby soon."

"Beth Ann, don't you forget that I'm your mama," the older woman said, and strolled back to the old colonial.

They were at the corner crosswalk that housed the old Art Deco Marine and Naval Hospital, built in the 1800s for injured seamen but now catering to the general public, including the mentally ill and elderly. "That's where we're going to be putting *her* soon," he said drily.

She slapped his tummy. "I might check *you* in first."

THE CLIFTON STATION OF THE SIRT sat on a tall trestle above Bay Street. The westbound concrete platform they were standing on had a brick tower that stood as a familiar pillar to those riding the train up to the North Shore.

As Dan had so many times before, and this afternoon he said it again: "This rapid transit ain't so rapid."

It actually was a beautiful ride. The dark green cars carried the legend *Staten Island* in gold. They took a seat on the maroon benches and started looking down the tracks to see if the train was close. She swung her legs back and forth as she looked at him.

"What are you thinking about?" he asked.

"About the last time," she whispered. "When that man brought out his rifle."

He stared at a crack in the pavement, wanted to respond, but didn't know what to say. The heels of her shoes began to scuff the concrete. Staten Island was an all-around sleepy, suburban community, especially at one o'clock in the afternoon on a weekday. One could hear a pin drop.

He was about to say something when the train came rolling in, and they got up to board it.

The doors slid open. The operator, pleasantly plump and bald, made sure they were on board. Beth Ann sat down on an orange seat facing south, the direction the train was going, and Dan sat flush against the wall, facing her. If you were drunk or squinting, the seats looked like Creamsicles with their glossy plastic finish and color.

They liked to use the time on the train to fine-tune their approach or at least discuss it. Beth Ann was fidgeting with the fringes of the brown suede pull-string purse in her lap. "How 'bout I wipe my forehead or cross my arms in vexation?" she asked.

Dan rolled his eyes. "That don't ever work. People don't want you looking nervous and stuff. We'll do the super-friendly-but-lost thing to get us goin'."

The train slowed to a screeching stop. The next stop after Clifton was Grasser, and the only person waiting on that platform to board was a tall, very old woman with a plastic see-through floral cap over her head and an old, beat-up brown dress that she had tried to dress up with a ragged green sweater. She had brown leather jacket boots with thick laces that looked as if she had no intention of ever taking them off, or maybe they were the only pair of shoes that she owned. She looked troubled and sad as she sat directly across from them with her back turned. She had a large shopping bag from E.J. Korvette's, a local staple that sold everyday clothes for kids and adults.

Five minutes later, the woman said loudly, "Ya know, my grandson was one of the workers that got killed back in February in the gas tank explosion in Bloomfield." She stated this as if she were reciting a homily, stern and loose at the same time. Beth Ann and Dan could see the frustration and sorrow in her face.

"I read about that in the paper," Dan said. "Forty workers killed, and they been protesting against them tanks for some time. It's a damn shame."

Beth Ann added, "I'm sorry to hear about your grandson. How old was he?"

"Only twenty-two. Didn't wanna go up to college on the hill like his brothers. He insisted on workin'." She had a cadence in her voice that was melodic and hit one's heart when heard. She seemed to be a very old soul as well as old—all-knowing.

"I hope he went right back up onto Jesus. At that age, he was still a baby. He hadn't lived much at all."

Beth Ann turned her whole body toward her and said, "I will pray for him, ma'am."

"Thank you, dear. You're a good woman."

The train came to another screeching halt at the New Dorp Train Station, and the old woman lifted her bag and left. As the doors closed behind her Dan looked at Beth Ann and said, "You ready?"

"I was born ready."

2.

It was still cool, and Connie had decided to blanch the tomatoes her father had grown in the yard. She loved to make tomato sauce from scratch, and anytime she had a day off from work, she took the opportunity to cook. From the white cabinet with the red knobs, she had pulled the white ceramic bowls she'd had her father order from the hardware store on Victory Boulevard. The family had moved to Justin Avenue from the Gravesend area of Brooklyn a few years back, along with some other families on the block. At the white ceramic sink that had been there when they moved in, she began to wash two red ceramic coffee cups and two red ceramic plates.

Brooklynites were used to having what was known colloquially as "coffee and cake" at five p.m. every day. It was almost like having English tea and scones at four, but it had been adapted to include "brown" coffee, and, typically, a store-bought Entenmann's cake. Connie's mother, Tina, had had her friend Domenica over the day before and left those dishes to the side. Domenica came from Palermo, in the same part of Sicily.

Connie's hands were large but delicate and well-kept. She had recently purchased a nude nail polish at the Duane Reade near her office and had her little sister paint her nails for when she returned to work. She wore 18-karat gold bangle bracelets that were taking on the shape of her wrist and that she rarely removed, not even to bathe.

She scrubbed the dishes quickly and efficiently, and placed them on the Formica countertop next to the stove, knowing that her mother would be asking for them later in the day.

Cooking was one of the only things that truly relaxed Connie's mind. She had left her heart in the old country and ruminated about her time there. She was twenty-three years old and had a position in the Alitalia Airlines ticket office. This had given her the opportunity to travel to her homeland at almost no cost whatsoever, and she loved that about her job.

She enjoyed traveling to the city every day to window-shop, exploring other parts of the world, and selling tickets to those eager to see her beautiful country. Her parents had bought the house in Staten Island a few years back and, although it was residential and quiet, her mother had been much happier in Brooklyn. She had been able then to walk to her favorite stores and go food shopping, and had had many more friends that were from various parts of Italy and spoke her language.

But her father Vittorio, a tile layer and real estate purchaser, had trouble hanging onto his money. He was heavy-handed when it came to the bottle and had made some bad choices when he bought real estate.

He had begun laying tile for Joe Manfredi, whom he had met in the real estate game. Manfredi had convinced him to buy the Staten Island house, and there had been no changing his mind. Vittorio was proud of the property and spoke about the additions that they had been making to the place ever since. He was especially proud of his brand-new Philips color television, which he kept boasting about to everyone. It was one of the newer models that had a brown wood furniture box encasing the screen. The right side of the box had silver knobs and dials. Connie caught him repeating himself about it to the neighbors, especially after he'd had a few drinks.

The drinking had taken a toll on the family, and Connie felt hurt by the things he did. She'd begun to attend a woman's group in Manhattan after work. The point of it was to have women take control of their own lives and not be afraid to explore avenues that were generally geared towards men. They would encourage women to apply for supervisory positions and gave tips on how to remain calm and confident in professional environments. It had given her a platform to express some of the challenges that she faced at work. She also considered it an equalizer between herself and other Americans, especially those of other races. She wanted to be accepted and live a full life in the States. She attended these meetings for herself; she didn't feel that she could discuss them freely at home.

"Where's Daddy today?" asked Lenore as she ran back into the kitchen to hang up the yellow rotary phone with the extremely long cord on the wall. Connie turned up the dial on their radio, which was brand-new and bright green. Her mother had left the Italian station on, and "*Chi Non Lava Non Fa L'amore*," by Adriano Celentano, was playing. She began humming the song as she got ice cube trays out of the freezer.

Lenore, Connie's little sister, was quite a few years younger and the only American-born member of the family. Connie said in a sinister murmur, "God only knows." Then, louder, "He's been doing a job for Mr. Manfredi in Clifton for weeks now."

At that moment the front door swung open, and Vittorio came through it humming and carrying a box of pastries from Alfonso's Bakery. He came in and said, "Putta these *nel frigo per tu mamma*." When Connie grabbed them from him, she could smell the vodka on his breath. He stumbled as he gave them to her. The box was white and tied neatly with green-and-white bakery string. He sloppily placed his hand on Lenore's head, rubbed it, and stumbled out of the kitchen into the basement.

Lenore looked up at Connie as she came back from the fridge and, disappointed, said, "I'm going to finish watching *Bonanza* in the living room."

3.

The train again jolted at Bay Terrace and stopped. Beth Ann and Dan made their way off onto the platform that had no overarch but the blue sky and fresh open air. There were plenty of times when the friendly operator would yell down an endearing greeting to the locals walking by under the train trestle, such as, "Save me a hot dog!" or "Did you see the Yankees lost the game last night?" Many of them were on the same shifts day in and day out. Staten Island was a small community, and the people all knew a familiar face when they saw one.

But Beth Ann and Dan seemed to be the only souls getting off the train. The operator looked out the window and asked, "You need any help gettin' around today?" They were not the types who frequented the area, and no local would overlook that without asking.

Beth Ann slyly turned, looked at him, and said with a

smile, "We're just visiting some friends. Finally my hubby and I have an afternoon to spend together. You know how shift workin' can be, don't you?"

The train operator nodded. "Yes, ma'am. Just askin'. Sometimes it's hard to find your way around down here, that's all. You and your husband enjoy your day."

The train began to move as Beth Ann and Dan hopped down the trestle steps to Justin Avenue and North Railroad. She grabbed his arm lovingly and whispered, "Look both ways before crossing, and look like you're lost. These Eyetalians have a tendency to look out their window."

They came to a stop and began to look up the street, east and west on the railroad line, and down the road behind them. They made their way up to a house on Justin Avenue, one of those newly built vernacular homes—part brick and part sided, with a white-cat house ornament running up the front of it. The door was white and had 62 in gold numbers on it.

Beth Ann checked her outfit, adjusted her pants, and slipped the kerchief off her head. She looked Dan up and down, too, gave him a peck on the cheek, and said, "I'm following your lead."

He knocked on the door. A moment later, a rambunctious eleven-year-old girl answered, looked at them oddly at first, then said, "Well, hello." Her hair was long and black, as were her eyes. She was wearing a red sweater with dark blue corduroy bell bottoms and a pair of blue Adidas sneakers. She glanced at the sofa behind her and said, "Con, there are people at the door that we don't know."

Dan quickly chuckled, "Oh, honey, no, *no*. . .we didn't mean to scare you. It's just that we were supposed to be meeting some friends down the road at North Railroad, but they don't seem to be home. We were thinking maybe their doorbell wasn't working, or that we went to the wrong address. We was just wondering if you'd be kind enough to let us use your phone."

A tall, pretty woman appeared at the door—about five-seven, with ash blonde hair and penetrating green eyes. He could see she was shy and sensitive from her delicate demeanor and soft, ladylike voice—not what you usually saw in the neighborhood. He figured she maybe worked somewhere in Manhattan. She was wearing a green dress that had a tie around the waist, nude high heels, and a gold locket that lay mid- chest.

"Hi. Sure you can come in and use the phone. We were just sitting down watching some TV."

Past a small entranceway, they entered the living room. There was a china cabinet to the right, the smaller doors on the sides of which were beveled; the center section had wire over the glass. Inside, he noticed statuettes, espresso cups, china dishes, and what looked like crystal glasses. To the right of it sat the newest Philips TV on the market, on a small table. *Bonanza* was on, and there was a scent of tomato sauce in the air, as if someone had just finished cooking some spaghetti. They had wall to wall off-white carpeting, too, and there was a silk-covered couch and a matching chair.

The younger, energetic sister said, "Can you believe that we're sisters? We're twelve years apart."

The older one mussed the younger's hair in anxiousness and asked their visitors to sit down. "Make yourselves comfortable. I'll get you the phone."

As they sat in front of a small coffee table, Beth Ann nudged Dan—code to notice what was on top of it: a nineteenth-century porcelain, glazed in pastel tones, of a woman sitting in a chair. The woman looked like Marie Antoinette. The piece had been broken into three pieces and left there to be repaired. Maybe one of the girls was going to glue it.

The older sister picked up a rotary phone from behind the TV and gave it to Dan.

He laid it down on the coffee table and said, "Thank you, miss."

Beth Ann at that moment asked the little sister, "So, sweet, where do you go to school around here?"

"St. Charles School, off of Hylan Boulevard. I only have another few years before I graduate." She slid to the floor and sat Indian style centimeters away from the TV while *Bonanza* ended.

Dan looked up at the older sister. "Ya know, we was on

Forest Avenue the other day and we came across one of these statues in that store that the old woman Edith Susskind owns. She got herself a nice collection of porcelain, don't she?" He smiled at the older sister in a way that perplexed her.

She quickly said, "Yes, we're familiar with her. . .I think it would be best if you just call your friends now—they must be waiting."

Beth Ann said, "Ya know, I noticed that locket you have on around your neck. It was shining right into my eyeball when you opened the door." She rose from the couch and approached her, smiling and looking straight into her eyes. The older sister gasped and began to shake.

At that moment, an old man in a white tank top, black slacks, and a ramshackle leather belt, humming an old Sicilian folk song, came up into the living room from the basement.

To his surprise, two black strangers were in his living room with his daughters. He stopped humming and asked, "*Who*-a these-a people in-a my-a *house?*"

Beth Ann turned from admiring the older sister's necklace and turned on her sweet voice, "Why, hello Mr. . .I'm sorry, what's your last name?"

"My name is Vittorio. It's-a no matter what *my* name is. Who-a *you?*"

She began to giggle. "Sir, I'm sorry. We didn't mean to

alarm you. Your lovely daughters were nice enough to let us in to use your phone. Ya see, we were visiting some friends, and they weren't answering their door, so we wanted to give them a call."

At that point, the older sister said, "Well, I think you've overstayed your welcome, and it's time for you to go now."

Dan rose from the couch and approached her with one hand in his pocket. "Why you doing *that* now, girl? There's no reason to act that way—but I could *give* you one." He pulled a knife with a tortoise shell handle from his pocket. She screamed, and he wrapped an arm around her neck and pressed the flat of the blade against her lips. Her green eyes turned turquoise as they welled up with tears.

Lenore started screaming at the top of her lungs. Beth Ann grabbed her and told her that if she didn't stop she would regret it.

The old man had run into the living room, looking for the phone in its usual spot. At that moment, Dan removed the knife from the older sister's lips, still holding her by the neck, and lunged at the old man with his knife just as the front door swung open. He had them both in a choke hold. A woman in her forties in a black-and-white shift dress and silver flats came through it. Patting her hair as if she had just come from the beauty parlor, she entered the living room, began to scream. Lenore twisted out of Beth Ann's hold and began screaming, "*Help, please help!*" and sobbing incessantly.

Beth Ann and Dan glanced at one another. He released Connie and Vittorio. Dan then grabbed the remnants of the broken statue on the table, and pushed Connie onto the couch and unplugged the TV. He swung the knife at the woman who had just entered. The old man fell to the floor in shock as Connie ran to the woman on the floor. Lenore started shrieking into the receiver again as Beth Ann and Dan flew out the front door and down the street under an open blue sky.

4.

Connie and her mother were both trying to get to their feet, crying hysterically. Victor had stumbled into the kitchen and opened the refrigerator, where Connie had the pastries he brought home. He kept an ice bucket on the same shelf, managed to drink a fifth of Gordon's every few days. His hands were shaking, and Lenore was standing in the doorway with tears streaming down her face. He told her to get the ice bags from underneath the sink in the downstairs bathroom.

The Italian radio was still playing Claudio Villa's *"Luna Rosa"* in the background, and the yellow rotary phone was off the hook. Lenore made her way down the stairs and back, her long black hair behind her, wiping her nose when she handed him the ice bags. He motioned to her. "Call-a the *poleece again!*"

She picked up the phone, hung it up, picked it up again, and dialed "0". The new emergency line, 9-1-1, was just emerging, and not everyone knew about it. When she got the operator, she began to stammer through her tears, and it was obvious that she was in a state of panic, "Hi, t-this is an emergency, we've been r-robbed, and my mother and sister have been injured. P-please send the police to 62 Justin Avenue *right away*."

She and her father continued to shove ice into the ice packs as Connie entered the kitchen, her eyes half closed, still crying hysterically. "Mommy's bleeding from her head!"

"Is okay, is okay," he said. "No cry. The police come now. Everything okay."

5.

Three Dodge Coronet police cars were rounding the corner of Justin Avenue and North Railroad as Beth Ann and Dan approached it. By then, exhaustion had set in, and they looked like they were about to pass out. The fringes on Beth Ann's bag had ripped when she left the Italians, and the gold bracelet from a previous job was dangling from it. She was unable to gather herself together when she saw the cars, her vision fuzzy and unclear, her breathing short, and she suddenly felt a nervous surge flow through her. Dan was sweating profusely, unable to settle himself. He saw her stumble and reached for her arm.

At that moment, two stocky police officers, both light-haired and light-eyed, came up with handcuffs, and one began to Mirandize them. "Do you understand the rights I have just read to you?" he asked when he had finished. "With these rights in mind, do you wish to speak to me?"

They both remained silent as the other cop murmured into his walkie-talkie, "Yeah, these are the ones been suspect for over a year now."

As they hustled them to the cars, she began to projectile vomit. An ambulance pulled up. The cop shoved her small and fragile body onto the grass and was applying pressure to her head when the EMTs rushed to the front door of the Italian family's home. The entire neighborhood had made its way onto their balconies by then, their front doors and steps, and were taking it all in.

6.

Connie composed herself because she knew she was going to be the only one who could communicate with the cops. The EMTs were trying to see whether her mother was lucid. "Miss? Miss, please squeeze my right arm if you see the light shining into your eye."

She had been slipping in and out of consciousness since she fell. Vittorio was standing over the EMTs, making sure that they were doing the best that they knew how. Lenore had been telling herself not to sob, but it sounded as if she had begun to hyperventilate again as she sat on the couch and watched.

A detective came in along with two young police officers, flashed his badge, and said evenly, "I'm Detective Noonan." He was in his late forties, tall and lanky, his eyes green, and he had crows' feet. His lips were thin and puckered. He didn't have cigarettes, but you could see a package of Big Red Gum through the pocket holder of his light-blue button-down shirt. He seemed comfortable and kind, as if such scenes were natural settings for him and he was going to take charge. "Are you the daughter of Vittorio Spatile?" he asked, glancing at a slip of paper he pulled from his shirt pocket.

She wondered how he knew the name. ". . .Yes," she said.

"Is this your father right here?"

"Well, yes," she replied in a confused and altered tone.

"Okay. Well, young lady, these two gentlemen are going to ask you some detailed questions about what happened here today. As for your father, he'll be coming down to the police station with me, and I'll be asking him a few questions myself."

She immediately pointed out that her father didn't speak English too well, and that she would appreciate it if he could stay at home while he was being questioned.

He studied her with an unassuming, concerned look and said, "Honey, I don't think that you're ready to hear the kinds of questions I'm going to have to ask your daddy today."

She didn't know how to respond to that, didn't think much of it, figured it was maybe some protocol that the cops had to follow. She wanted to make sure that they knew what had happened, and that the thieves were prosecuted for the crime. She turned to her father and said, *"L'ufficiale di polizia vuole portarti a interrogare, vai con lui."*

He looked up and—when the EMT assured him that his wife would be on her way to Richmond Memorial Hospital— nodded and stepped toward the detective.

She had been anxious when she said it, because on days when he got home early, he would begin drinking around two o'clock in the afternoon, his words slurring by dinner. She knew all about his infidelity and alcoholism, and that was part of why she had joined the woman's group—to find a better life and future for herself without the hassle of having to rely on a man to support her. But she wasn't thinking about that just then: She wanted to make sure that the thieves paid for what they had done.

As her father and the detective left her home and her mother was taken out on a stretcher to the hospital, Connie made sure that Lenore would stay with Carmine across the street for a little while. Carmine was a large woman in her mid-forties whose husband, Anthony, owned a carpet installation company and worked hard to support his little family. He had installed *their* carpet a few years back and done a great job. She had two older sons and a daughter, Jackie, who was the same age as Lenore. She had always been a bit of a noisy neighbor, but her character went well with her size—large and innocent. She had been standing outside when they took Tina into the ambulance, and she gave Connie a big hug.

Carmine's teeth were split in the middle and bucked, and she was always chewing a very white piece of gum that would flop in and out of her mouth. Her hair was curly, her skin a lovely olive, and when she approached you, you felt safe. It was as if she had a natural calm that made you feel everything was going to be swell. "There are some crazy tickets on this island, let me tell you," she said.

Connie, instantly reassured, began to cry out all the stress and asked her to take Lenore for a few hours.

Carmine obliged willingly, said that she was welcome to stay with them as long as she'd like, even spend the night if she wanted to.

Connie guided the police into the kitchen and sat them down where she had left the tomatoes to become soft and unusable, lying in a bowl of ice next to the dirty dishes. They sat around the yellow Formica table in the yellow cushioned vinyl chairs, and she reached into one of the cabinets for an ash tray as a courtesy. She wanted to make sure that she was being as polite as possible.

The questions they asked her were objective and led to what they suspected. One of the cops was twenty-seven and had brown hair, brown eyes, and a name tag that read

Battaglia. His nose was almost as wide as his face, and he had big, green eyes that resembled pretty fish.

The other, named McCormick, was a few years younger and had ash blond hair and a voice that expressed unexpected sensitivity and kindness.

Battaglia asked, "Did they approach the door like they were lost and needed to use the phone?"

"Yes."

"They say that they were visiting friends?"

"Yes, they did."

McCormick cleared his throat. "And they told you they needed to use the phone?"

She nodded. "That's right."

"Did they sit themselves down when they came into the living room?"

"Uh-huh."

The cops glanced at each other. "Yep, that's them," said Battaglia. "They been pulling the same spiel at a number of households all over the island for about year now." He leaned over to answer his walkie-talkie. It was Officer Noonan. They were going to "keep Vittorio in the slammer overnight for further questioning."

Connie didn't think she'd heard that correctly. She waited for them to give her the message. Battaglia turned back to her and noticed that she had her hands pressed to both sides of her forehead.

"They're—uh, they're keeping your father at the precinct overnight, miss."

". . .Why?"

"We're going to have to wait and find out."

7.

Beth Ann and Dan were sitting in handcuffs in the glass room to the right at the 120th Precinct in Saint George, waiting for further directives from the cops, when their mother appeared at the door. "Mama, how's you know we were here?"

Clarice removed a handkerchief from underneath her right sleeve and wiped the tears from her face. As she looked over at them, she couldn't believe her eyes. Her heart sank, and she wanted to say something, to enter the room that they were in, but she stood still and felt frozen. They were sitting across the room, leaning against the pasty blue walls, with battered, open wounds on their faces, and looking at her exasperated and desperate.

The words wouldn't make their way out of her mouth, but she wanted to keel over. As she was about to say something, Noonan appeared and asked her to come with him.

She did so. They made their way to a swinging maple Dutch door; Noonan held it open, his Wagner College ring shining on his finger, and escorted her to the back room, where Vittorio Spatile sat. They made eye contact with, Noonan noted, a look of familiarity.

At that moment, in a sudden fury, Clarice screamed, "Don't hurt my babies! What are you doing with *my babies?*" She turned to Noonan. "That man is *dangerous.* He got the woman that used to live in our building pregnant with a baby, and he pretend not to know it. That baby damn near two years old, and he do nothin' for it, not *nothin.*"

Noonan wrapped his arm around her and asked her to calm down. "Ma'am, I did not know that those two are your children, but they are being held on a charge of grand larceny. However, we are trying to find the woman and the baby that you are referring to. Do you know where they are currently residing?"

"Yes, I do!" She wept until the tears were pouring down her face.

8.

Connie pulled up the ramp and into the parking lot at Richmond Memorial Hospital. She entered through the sets of double doors and ran down the hallway, past plastic ramps lying flush against a wall covered with wall paper the color of sea foam with pink brush strokes. She found the front desk and said to a petite blonde in white scrubs, "I'm Tina Spatile's daughter? She was brought in a few hours ago, and she should be in Intensive Care."

The clerk said, almost as if she'd knew she was coming,

"Yes, miss. Take the elevator to the third floor and make a right. She's in room 3B. The doctors are waiting for you."

Connie hit the button on the antiquated elevator and waited for what seemed the longest thirty seconds of her life, trying not to reflect on the disaster she was living through.

A Dr. Volpe was standing by the door of 3B, talking to a nurse named Boyle who was writing down his orders. Connie introduced herself. "How is she?"

He said, "Hi," and smiled kindly. "You know what they say—be wary of smiling doctors." He laughed, and she felt a sense of relief. "There's nothing to worry about," he went on. "Your mother will make her way to a full recovery, and she has completely regained consciousness. We're doing some memory tests, though, and I think it may be best if you come back tomorrow to see her. This way, some of the shock may lessen and we can prepare her for visitors. I'll let her know you were here."

Connie felt a surge of anger. "I have to attend to an urgent matter, but I'll be back here to spend the night, even if I have to sleep in the lobby downstairs."

"Do as you must. Just know that she's in good hands here with us."

She thanked him and, as she walked down the hall, found the down staircase. She quietly made her way to the front lobby, glanced at the clerk, said, "Good evening," and walked out the door. She had reached a state of exhaustion that was irreversible, but she managed to get in the car. When the cops left her house, they'd told her where her father would be.

She drove quickly from the South Shore to the North, found the precinct, and parked illegally on Water Street. Her Le Sportsac tote was worn from traveling, but she liked the compartments. She reached into the inside zipper pocket and pulled out her ID, knowing that she would have to show proof before entering the place. Just past the double doors, she turned left and ran into Detective Noonan standing against the front desk, hand reaching over the podium, and yelling into the phone, "I have *two* perps sittin' here, and I do *not* know what case to begin with first—they're *separate issues.*" At that moment, he turned around and calmed down when he saw Connie standing outside the swinging Dutch door. "Listen," he went on, "I gotta go. I'll talk to you later."

He hung up the phone, walked over to her, and said, "Miss, what I'm about to reveal is going to change your life for good."

She didn't know what to think of it. She couldn't handle any more stress, but he took her arm and calmly guided her to the window-paned interrogation room. She looked in. There were her father, sitting speechless, Clarice crying, and what looked to be a seventeen-year-old girl and a small, beautiful child.

As Noonan walked Connie into the room, the young

woman looked up and asked, "What in God's name are you doing? Why do you insist on bringing more people into this?"

Connie didn't know what to make of what she was seeing. Detective Noonan looked and studied her for a long moment before he told her, "It's all of us, not just you—and it's all a part of growing up."

ORPHEUS

A T EDINBORO ROAD, THE TOURISTS, almost all from Japan, made their way off the Greyhound that had brought them to the house. If one were to take a birds eye view of Lighthouse Hill from Arthur Kill Road, they would see the beautiful structure positioned against the lighthouse.

The short, lanky bus driver, who was wearing very thick glasses, had driven up the hill that held the beautiful homes, the Tibetan Museum, and the Lighthouse. He had doubled as a tour guide and pointed out in a nasal voice over the loud-speaker, after wiping his nose and clearing his throat, "We are now approaching Crimson Beech, designed by Frank

Lloyd Wright for builder Marshall Erdman in 1959. He died right before he saw the final product. It was his last project. Ms. Cass, the owner of the house, will be hosting a tour for one dollar per person; however, if you don't want to pay the dollar, you can enjoy the surrounding grounds of the house. Please be mindful of the privacy of the other residences on the hill. Thank you."

There was a young man on the bus who seemed out of place. He stepped off the bus onto the dirt road after all the others had departed—six foot four, in white loafers and a blue leisure suit. He approached the driver and shook his hand, "I am Horace Handforth, how are you?" He had an injured knee and walked with a limp. His hair was blonde, and he stood erect, confident in his way. He could not have been a day over twenty-six, but he had the demeanor of an older man. Horace had a rigid briefcase in his right hand and asked the driver, "What part a town are we entering here?"

"These parts here are what they call Richmondtown. If you make your way down the road a bit, some of the locals have preserved the area like it was at the turn of the century and before. If you're interested, ask to speak to a Mr. Shepard—he'll help you get around."

Horace thanked him but mentioned that he was going to meet some family and wanted to make sure that he was in the right place. "Have a good day, sir. I won't be seeing you on the way back, so please don't wait up!"

He walked away, making sure that he was going in the right direction, far behind the tourists.

Ms. Catherine Cass, an attractive woman in her late thirties, had short brown hair that might have been curled with cushioned wire rollers. Her green eyes were light and endearing, and they were in keeping with her soft-spoken manner. She had a woven basket in her hand, the kind church ushers pass around when they collect donations. She was wearing a navy blue pleated skirt with a white silk button-down shirt, smiling, waiting stoically in the enclave outside the front door, to welcome the Japanese people into her home. As all fifteen of them approached, they looked sullen and tired, yet once they saw her welcoming face, they seemed relieved.

Horace made his way to the neighbor's home. There were steps on the side of the house. They were green and earthy, as if they had emerged out of the landscape like a natural passageway to an underground world.

Two olive-skinned teenage girls, with long brown hair and brown eyes, were sitting on them. They were giggling and engaged in some frivolous conversation. At that moment, they glanced over at him.

He had not expected to see them there, and his self-assured attitude and inscrutable manner crumpled at once. He flinched and caught himself almost cowering, losing his composure at the sight of the young ladies. Trying to recover, he said, "Sorry to descend on you so abruptly! I didn't mean to scare you." He reached for the soft pack of Camels in one pants pocket, then for the lighter in the other, pulled out a cigarette with his lips, and asked, "Either of you young ladies like a smoke?"

They batted their big brown eyes, looked at one another, and the younger of the two said, "Sure, we'll both have one."

2.

Early the next morning, just before sunrise, Eunice and Corinne Cass, laid in their beds in the Frank Lloyd Wright house. They shared a room. It was modern and wood-paneled with sharp edges and pointed corners. As they lay awake, they couldn't say enough about what they both liked about Horace and what it was that made him so mysterious, but it was awakening something inside them.

Eunice twirled her hair when she got nervous or excited, and it was difficult in the quiet hours to not hear her fingernails tapping against one another with each twirl, as if she were about to lay deep into herself at any moment. "Do you think he thought I was pretty?" asked Eunice. She was the younger of the two sisters and starting her junior year of high school.

Corrine rolled her eyes and made a face. "Yeah, I'm sure he did think you were pretty and he's looking to charm his way into the life of someone who doesn't know anything about him." She knew how driven and anxious her little sister could be, and how impressionable. She herself had always been more jaded, seeing things as they were, not as they seemed.

Horace had mentioned to them that he was staying with the Handforths. The Handforths were the Cass's neighbors and lived in what was known to be the Platt House. They had once had a farm in Nova Scotia, but the Nova Scotians did not approve of an Englishman marrying a French woman, so one day a group of neighbors burned down their farm along with their livestock. They then made their way to Staten Island.

Corrine, reserved and keeping her cool that afternoon, had embraced what Horace was saying. They had all got to talking on the steps and came to know that he was a learned and experienced man. As he continued to smoke his cigarette, a sudden preoccupation came over him and he asked, "Have you ever heard of Aeschylus?" Corrine calmly responded with, "I think so, wasn't he a Greek writer?"

Horace looked at them and said, "Yeah, yeah he was." He wrote something once that has always stayed with me, as he looked off and zoned out he quoted: *"And even in our sleep, pain which cannot forget falls drop by drop upon the heart, until in our own despair, against our will, comes wisdom through the awful grace of God."*

Corinne had been thinking about what he said ever since he said it and trying to apply it to her life. She had been thinking about her long-time boyfriend, Bobby. Since she started Carnegie Mellon last fall she hadn't really seen much of him though. The safeness that she felt with Bobby remained seductive, but she was afraid that it wouldn't withstand the new experiences and rapid growth that she was experiencing at school. Now that the stranger had said what he had, she wondered where this uncertainty would lead her and she was now just as intrigued with Horace as her sister, though would not admit it.

Corrine laid under the pink duvet cover with the white silk trim, staring at the ceiling. To the left, under the window, stood an immovable desk that had been placed there by the late Frank Lloyd Wright. Eunice's blue-and-white pompoms hung over it. Also on the desk laid their lava lamp, their old Raggedy Anne doll, and the imitation *I Dream of Jeannie* vase with different-colored sand in it. Eunice was a baton twirler at Susan Wagner High School and she followed in her sister's baton twirling footsteps.

The small transistor radio in the kitchen was turned to *1010 Wins* and the newscaster announced that the new governor Mario Cuomo would be speaking later in the day. Although Eunice remained preoccupied with her hair-twirling and thoughts, Corrine turned her attention to the radio. Their mother had been an education advocate on the community board since they moved to Staten Island ten years ago and Corrine had a passing interest in the policy making as well. Their mother was up at the crack of dawn every morning making breakfast at 5 am and listening adamantly to *1010 WINS.* The girls could hear it all the way from their bedroom.

Mr. Cass would get up at 6:00 a.m. every morning and make his way to the kitchen. No matter what was playing on the radio, he would embark upon his morning ritual and begin to listen to his *Rembetika,* Greek folk music that stemmed from the forced immigration of two million Greeks out of Asia Minor. His hands were large, his face sweet but stern. He had a small, thin mustache and large lips well proportioned to the other features of his face. His eyes were dark and beady but expressed intense passion when you spoke to him. He was having breakfast while he looked over the stocks in the morning paper. His back had been hurting since he had gotten permission to install a pool on the property after submitting all the proper documentation. It was easier to do now that Frank Lloyd Wright was dead.

Once a week, Ms. Cass would prepare Loukoumades, Greek donuts with honey. He would enjoy them with some Turkish coffee in a demitasse cup. His hands got sticky from the honey and caught on his thin mustache. Mr. Cass would then lick his fingers and twirl his mustache. There were times when he got angry at himself because the honey caught on the paper and the girls would hear him cursing himself under his breath.

Corinne knew mornings were not the best time to approach him. She'd been trying to talk him into buying some art from some of the newly emerging Pop artists, like Basquiat and Keith Haring. She was taking a course on modern art at school, and her art teacher had been trying to get his work into a gallery in Soho. He'd mentioned up-and-coming painters growing popular, but still affordable. Her last conversation with him on this topic had not gone well.

"Dad," she had said, "if we buy some of these paintings, they might be worth millions of dollars one day. These people are up and coming with something new to offer."

"It's too much of a risk," he had said. "We already own this house, and it'll be worth plenty. Now leave me alone."

Mr. Cass owned a well-established employment agency in Manhattan and had decided to make the move to Staten Island from Corona, Queens after his little boy passed away. One evening while in bed, Mr. Cass and his wife were watching an interview Mike Wallace was having with Frank Lloyd Wright. They were discussing the emergence of pre-fabricated homes, and Frank Lloyd Wright had mentioned the deal that he had struck to design a few in the Northeast.

Bill Cass had glanced at his wife that evening with an idea. Catherine had been tired, worn, and drained. He could see it in her eyes, and he wanted to see her become her whole self again.

He had always known that she could write and was a

charming communicator. The trauma of the loss, and the ever-growing population in Queens, had led him to say, "Write him a letter and tell him we're interested."

Her immediate reaction had been, "Bill, you got to be crazy."

3.

Ms. Cass and the girls were enjoying the summer sun in the yard. Ms. Cass was humming to herself as she made arrangements in a vase with some of the roses that she'd grown in the garden.

"So I heard that decentralization of the system is not producing the results the feds wanted to see, Mom." Corrine said as she sunbathed on the lawn. She was idly flipping through a clothing catalog while Eunice lay on her belly next to her looking at a Seventeen magazine. Suddenly, the door to the yard opened and Hannah Handforth bustled out. Hannah was their next door neighbor and a woman no taller than five foot three, but you wouldn't know it. She had a "tall" personality. Thin and polished, she had a short blonde bob, blue eyes, and a button nose. "Cathy, are you there?" Hannah bellowed in a vaudevillian timbre.

Cathy, always pleased to see Hannah Handforth, turned from the patio table to the door. "Hi, Hannah!" she called out and gave her a hug and kiss. "What brings you here? Are the girls driving you crazy again with their late-night parties?"

The girls rose from their sun-bathing position and greeted Hannah as well.

"Oh, no, no—I wanted to ask you a big, big favor," Hannah replied. She brought her hands together in front of her white shorts and plaid, button-down shirt. "It's just that my nephew, Horace, is visiting, and ya see, he's had some unexpected personal issues these past few years and had been staying with his mother. But my sister felt things weren't happening for him at home and she suggested he come down here and stay with me for a while." She leaned in closer to Cathy and said almost in a whisper, "She's hoping New York can be more stimulating for him."

"Well, I would certainly think so," Cathy said. Corrine listened with rising curiosity, her first meeting with Horace was still very fresh in her mind.

Hannah continued, "I'm inclined to ask if maybe he could accompany you to one of those board meetings that you go to, so he can do some networking and maybe get to know some other educators. Before his troubles he was an accomplished English teacher and had a real love of the subject. I think it might do him some good."

"Well, of *course*, I'd love to," Cathy said, "but I'm afraid I won't be able to make the next one. It's this Wednesday night and I have to be at the Rotary Club."

"I could accompany him," Corrine suggested.

"Are you sure honey, you don't have to," Cathy said.

"No, it's fine. I'd like to go and see what it's all about."

"I'd like to go too," Eunice chimed in.

Corrine gave her a sideways look. "It wouldn't interest you."

"How do you know?"

"Because it has nothing to do with hair spray and lipstick."

"I'm old enough to know what's going on."

Corrine turned to her mother and Mrs. Handforth, "Excuse me, I have to get ready for my date with Bobby. I'll be out in a bit and we'll make some plans." She went back into the house

Horace had then made his way to the yard and looked uneasy and awkward. He looked as if he had just woken up despite it being almost two in the afternoon. Ms. Cass immediately sensed his tension and welcomed him with open arms. She approached him and said, "Hello, it is so nice to meet you. So, I heard you're a teacher?"

He looked at her, his shoulders moved from an uptight position to a more relaxed one. He responded with, "Yes, I have taught in a few states now. I haven't been in the classroom for about a year though."

Ms. Cass nodded and then kindly said, "Come and sit down, we'll talk. I just made some lemonade. Your Aunt and I have been neighbors for many years, good ones."

Eunice then took the towel from under her, stood up and

wrapped the towel around herself with great ease and confidence. "Hey, we met the other day, what's up? I didn't know you were Mrs. Handforth's nephew."

He looked at her and suddenly transmuted into a charming man with wandering eyes. He looked her up and down and said, "Yeah, I was a little tired from the trip up here."

Suddenly, Cathy spoke up as if she had just remembered something. "Hannah, have I showed you the new Tupperware I got at Nancy's the other night?" Nancy Purpura held a sales party every month for everyone in the neighborhood. She would sell jewelry, Tupperware or anything else that upper-class housewives felt they needed to decorate their houses with as symbols of their status to the rest of the neighborhood.

"No, but I'd love to see them," Hannah said. She followed Cathy into the house, leaving Horace and Eunice alone in the yard.

Eunice looked up at him and said, "Here, let's have some lemonade."

They went to the patio table and she poured them two glasses of lemonade and he began to look at her intently. Nothing was said between them for what seemed like several minutes and Eunice began to feel uncomfortable.

"So, what do you like to do around here for fun?" Horace finally asked.

Eunice perked up as this was something she knew how

to talk about. "There's lots of stuff. We usually go out to the mall and shop. Sometimes after school we go to the Victory Diner in Dongan Hills. You ever been there?"

"No."

"It's a great little diner. Looks like something from the sixties. I can take you there if you'd like."

"Maybe." Horace sipped the lemonade and continued to analyze Eunice. "How old are you?"

"I'm sixteen. Why?"

Horace shook his head absently. "Just curious. You look older. You can pass for twenty or twenty-one".

"Really?"

"Yes. You're very beautiful. You remind me a little of my wife."

Eunice blushed and looked down at the ground. "You're just saying that."

"No, I'm not. You really do. You have her eyes."

"What happened to her?"

Horace downed the rest of the lemonade and put the glass down hard on the patio table, startling Eunice. "So what grade are you in?"

"I'm going to be a junior."

He pulled a pack of cigarettes from his pocket and lit one up. "I used to teach juniors. I enjoyed it. They're too young to have their own ideas but old enough to appreciate the literature I had them read. What books do they have you reading in class?"

Eunice thought for a moment, "Well, last year we did Romeo and Juliet. I got to read Juliet's part in class. I don't understand why they had to both die. Seems like a waste. Then we read The Catcher in the Rye, but I didn't really like that one too much."

"How come?"

"I don't know, nothing much really happens and he just seems like a really unlikable person. It was kinda boring too." Eunice shrugged her shoulders and took another sip of lemonade. "But, I don't really know though."

Horace studied Eunice as the sun fell off her back, highlighting her hair. She looked fragile and vulnerable and reminded him of his wife more than ever.

"You know what," Horace said, "I thought it was boring too." He laughed and Eunice gave him a wide smile. "Say," he continued, "I was thinking of doing some exploring. Would you like to accompany me?"

Eunice moved her hair behind her ear, "Sure, that'll be fun. Where do you want to go?"

"I've never been to Manhattan."

"Manhattan? Sure, we can do that. The train goes right to the ferry. It's a nice ride."

Horace smiled, "Great. Let's do that."

"Cool. Just let me change, okay."

Eunice ran into the house and to her room. Corrine was

in the bathroom getting ready for her meeting with Bobby. She saw Eunice run past her from the vanity mirror.

"Hey, what are you in such a hurry for?"

Eunice was already out of her bathing suit and into a pair of jeans. "I'm taking Horace into Manhattan."

"You're doing what?" Corrine dropped her brush into the sink and it clanged around the porcelain. She went into Eunice's room. "What do you mean?"

"Horace asked if I could take him to look around Manhattan. He's never seen it. I said sure. We're taking the ferry."

"He asked you to go with him?"

"Yes." Eunice had put on a top and sneakers.

"Why would he ask you?"

Eunice shrugged as she applied lipstick in the closet mirror. "I don't know, maybe he finds me attractive."

"He doesn't."

"How do you know?"

"Because you're sixteen. What would he want to do with you? What could he possibly talk about?"

Eunice turned to look at Corrine. "He happens to think I'm much more mature for my age. He said so."

"He did?"

"Yep." Eunice returned her attention to the mirror, now applying mascara to her eyes.

Corrine shouldn't have cared that Eunice was going with Horace, but she did. Ever since she had first met him on the steps there was something about him that lingered in her head. It was the mysteriousness of him. She didn't want to admit it to herself but a part of her was jealous that Horace wanted Eunice to show him around. It was supposed to be her taking him. She was far more experienced and intellectual than her sister.

"You don't even know him," she said to Eunice.

"So. He's Mrs. Handforth's nephew and she's a close friend of mom's. Besides what do you care? Don't you have to see Bobby?"

Corrine had momentarily forgotten about Bobby and was now frustrated that she had to see him. The truth was despite how much Corrine liked Bobby, she had outgrown him. She felt it ever since she left Staten Island to go to college, but was just now realizing it. Bobby was a nice guy, but he was never getting off this island and Corrine knew it.

"Bobby's supposed to come by to pick me up. We can all go together into the city."

Eunice laughed out loud. "You think Bobby will want to go into Manhattan? Please."

Corrine knew he wouldn't. "Fine, but we'll take you to the ferry then."

"No, Horace wants to ride on the Staten Island Railroad. That's what we're gonna do."

"Okay, fine, but we'll drive you to the station. It's a long walk." Corrine walked out before Eunice could answer back.

4.

Bobby Gordon had been waiting at the side of his 1980 maroon Cadillac Deville. His nose was pudgy, and he had shoulder length curly hair and a goatee. Over bell bottom jeans and a *Susan Wagner High School Class of 1981* t-shirt that had what looked like a hot-dog float on the front of it, he had a tie-dyed jacket with black trim and goggle sunglasses. Peter Frampton's "Wind of Change" was playing on the car stereo. A social butterfly, Bobby was perplexed to see the tall, mysterious guy he had never laid eyes on before approaching the car.

"Hey, pretty lady," he said to Corinne. "How are you?"

She gave him a peck on the lips and fixed his glasses. "I'm doing well. Listen, we have to give my sister and Horace a ride to the train."

He looked over her shoulder. "Who's Horace?"

Horace fluttered a hand in the air. "I am. Horace Handforth. And you are. . . ?"

Bobby stood up straight as Corrine moved out of the way and rested an elbow on his shoulder. "Hey, I'm Bobby. Nice to meet you."

Eunice said facetiously, "Are you ever going to cut that hair?"

He lowered his glasses again and said sarcastically, "Nice to see you too, kid."

She laughed and winked as the sun shone on her face.

"Thanks for the ride," Horace said as he opened the door for her.

Eunice and Bobby had a little-sister-and-big-brother relationship, comfortable enough to make fun of each other. She hoped Corrine would never let him go. Bobby lived not too far away, in Castleton Corners at the bottom of Todt hill. His father was an English teacher at Curtis High, and his mother did clerical work at the Proctor and Gamble plant at Port Ivory in Mariners Harbor. They were happily married and loved Bobby to death. His dad made sure that he had everything he wanted and then some. He'd bought him the Caddy when he graduated high school and promised him he could have it if he attended Richmond College instead of going away. His parents were good to him, and he was loyal in return.

5.

They got in the car and drove back down the hill onto Meisner Avenue, past Egger Home, which led to Rockland Avenue that then became Arthur Kill Road. Horace had become quiet, captivated by the Greenbelt and the Richmondtown Reservation, while Bobby tried to entertain them all by talking a mile a minute and using his thumb and pinky to tap the steering wheel to the beat of the music.

"So my folks are at the house in Pennsylvania for a few weeks," he went on to say. "I think it'll be good if we have a few beers with the old gang in my yard."

Corrine rolled her eyes and had tried to turn the conversation when she realized that they were going in the wrong direction. "Bobby, you have to take them to the train!"

"Oh, yeah." He stepped on the brake and made a wide U-turn in the parking lot at Holtermann's Bakery.

Eunice told Horace that the Holtermanns had been family friends of theirs for a long time, and that she highly recommended their Cheese Danishes.

Horace asked, "Do you know any good bars around here?"

Eunice did not know how to respond. She only went to a bar once with her girlfriends last summer and it was attached to a restaurant. The bartender was their friend's older brother and he made them sit at the bar so he looked like he would have a crowd to attract paying customers. She laughed anxiously and said, "Not really."

"What do ya say?" asked Bobby, who never let go of anything. "I think it'd be nice to see Karen, Annie, Mark, and Paul."

"Listen," Corinne told him, "we'll talk about it later, okay? Not now."

Eunice and Horace got out at the station. Eunice leaned over and kissed Bobby on the cheek. "Thanks, babe. I'll hang out in your yard anytime."

He laughed and said, "Lushes aren't allowed."

Corinne said, "Okay, okay, *stop,* you two, before you begin bickering. The train should be here soon."

Eunice poked her head through the passenger window and said, "Have fun wherever you're going."

"We'll probably go to Jade Island," Bobby said.

Corrine rolled her eyes, "Again."

Bobby gave her an exasperated look. "It's the best Chinese on the island." Corrine and Bobby drove off, leaving Eunice and Horace alone on the street.

A small dive named The Players Place was on the street that led to the station entrance. Horace turned to Eunice and asked, "Do you want to stop in and get a beer before we get on the train?"

She thought that forward and strange—why would he ask her to do such a thing without knowing her at all?—but tried to played it cool. "Well, I like beer, but we'll miss the train. It's supposed to be coming in a few minutes."

Horace waved his hand at her. "So what, another will come shortly after. Come on, let's stop in for a little."

Eunice rubbed her arm. "I don't know."

"Just one drink, I promise. It's so hot today. I'll be good before we set out."

"Okay, just one," she said uneasily.

"Great! Let's *do* this." They made their way into the bar, where an older fellow with steel gray hair was working the counter. He looked up at Horace while he was wiping a highball dry. Horace said, "Hello again."

The bartender stopped wiping and replied with a trace of apprehension, "Hello. I hope all's well."

Horace and Eunice sat at the bar. She made sure that her dress and bag weren't dangling off the stool. Horace ordered two Rolling Rocks.

The bartender took off the bottle caps and said, "Here ya go, boss," and, before he gave Eunice hers, studied her seriously and added, "Am I sure that you're eighteen years of age, little lady?"

"Well, of course I am," she said, and smiled accordingly.

"This is my niece," Horace said. "I'm just taking her around town today. She's good to go."

"Okay," the bartender said and put the bottle down in front of her. Horace gave Eunice a wink.

He was now more chipper than he had been all day and he quickly sucked down his beer. An older gentleman who was standing idly next to a pool table under the window, waiting for someone to play, noticed him. Above the table hung what resembled a flying saucer on a long black string dangling from the ceiling, and, although the sun was still out, the light had been turned on and dimly lit it.

"Wanna play a game?" the older man asked Horace. He looked at Horace again, more closely, and soon realized he had seen him there before. He could not remember when, but was certain it had not been good.

Horace shook his head and said, "No, sir, not today—I

have a guest with me here." He asked Eunice, "Are you a fan of The Styx?"

"Yeah! I'm a *huge* fan!"

He laughed. "What's your favorite song?" and, without much hesitation, quickly added, "I like 'Babe'." He got up and went over to the jukebox. He took a coin out of his pocket and chose the song. It played through the speakers. He awkwardly danced his way back over to Eunice and sat down.

She giggled nervously. "I like this song, too."

"Good!" He waved to the bartender and ordered a shot of Jack Daniels.

"You said only one beer," said Eunice, "we have to catch the train."

He sighed. "Don't worry about it. . . . How do you think the afterlife goes?" He said it with real curiosity, as if he was really interested in what she had to say.

She absently grabbed a lock of hair and twirled it. "I-I think that—"

"Do you think that we come back to Earth again and again, or that we go to heaven or hell? What are your beliefs?"

Eunice shrugged and said sheepishly, "I haven't given it much thought. I guess I was raised to believe that we go to heaven or hell. . . . What makes you bring that up?"

He looked down at his shoes, hair hanging shaggily over his brow, a hand on his forehead. "Oh, it's just some thoughts that've been making their way through my mind for the past few months. I lost my wife a few years back in a car crash, you know, and the grief was. . .sudden and unexpected. It seems that I've gone down the rabbit hole a bit. I don't sleep much anymore. I just stay up and go for walks. I usually walk into bars." He stared off into space. "Everyone said it was going to take time, but all I remember is wanting to work, and I felt like I had to live for the both of us, even though she was no longer here. It's almost like I thought that she was coming back, denying what happened."

Eunice took note of his sadness. She didn't know what to say. "Well, you know that she wanted you with her, and that she didn't leave you."

His blue eyes met hers. "Yeah, I *have* said that to myself, again and again, but I still had these feelings of anger towards her and towards myself. I think, if I'd been home, she wouldn't have gone to the store. . .and what would have happened if she recovered? Why did she die?" He put his face in his hands.

The bartender served him the shot of Jack. He knocked it down and immediately asked for another. Eunice became increasingly more uncomfortable and began to look around the bar to see if there was a pay phone.

"Come on, Horace," she said. "Can we please just go. We don't even have to go to the city, I just want to go back home."

He ignored her. "Ya know, when I was in Maine last year,

I was really doing well for myself. I was thinking about writing a book, had a good sub gig at the local high school, and I thought I was moving on, but it didn't pan out."

She noticed that he was starting to slur his words and his eyes were getting weepy. He looked strange to her. At that moment, he turned to the man standing by the pool table and said, "Ya know, I'll play a game with you, Buddy." He stumbled his way to the pool table and grabbed a pool stick off the wall. "We meet last time?"

The old man said, "Yes, we did son."

After playing a game of pool and losing, he made his way back to the bar to sit next to Eunice who had been trying to avoid conversation with the bartender and the other bar patrons.

Horace looked at her. "Ya know my wife had pretty brown hair like yours and a big smile like yours."

He continued to look at her intently and more ferociously. He drew himself closer to her and put his hand on her pink cheek, caressing it. She got up out of the stool and said that she wanted to leave. He looked at her and said, "Well, why? The party is just getting started."

6.

As they got out of the car, Bobby and Corinne started to feel a mutual awkwardness that stemmed from when they had seen each other over spring break. One night while they were at Brandy's Pond, at their girlfriend Patty's house for a party, they'd got to talking, and Corinne had told him she didn't think they should see each another anymore.

He had clearly been hurt but hadn't said much, just looked at her straight in the face and asked, "Are you with someone else?"

Tears had begun to stream down her face. "No, I'm still in love with you, but I don't think this works." They'd packed up their things, and he had taken her home. It was the longest and most silent ride they could have taken, but they had parted ways without knowing what to make of it.

Bobby had a strong personality and not a malicious bone in his body. He wanted to make light of the awkwardness. He looked at her. "I think you are pretty as ever."

She giggled and glanced back with nothing but disdain. "Ugh! Why do you make it impossible for me to. . . ."

"Yeah, yeah and all that jazz. I'm taking you to Jade Island."

They drove the rest of the way to the Chinese restaurant in silence. They pulled into the parking lot and made their way into what looked like a small Polynesian Island with a tiki bar and Polynesian music, bamboo décor, and a short Asian man waiting to greet them. The man knew Bobby and his family well. "How are you? How many tonight?"

"Doing well, and how are you? . . . Just two tonight, and thank you."

They were seated at a table with a white tablecloth, yellow cloth napkins, a candle in a yellow beveled votive, and a fresh pink-and-white calla lily in a white vase. Corinne laid her purse on the empty seat next to her and went to use the bathroom. When she came back, there were two demitasse cups and a silver tea kettle on the table. Bobby, who had been examining the menu, looked up at her with his eyes closed, but he couldn't delay it any longer. "How's school going?"

She didn't want to talk about it, but she had been up all night thinking and figured she'd start there.

"What do you think about overcoming obstacles?"

Confused, he shook his head. "Wait—what? Obstacles?"

"Just hear me out. I know it's a weird response, but what do you think about them when they come up?"

"I. . .I deal with them, I guess. What kind of obstacles are you talking about?"

"Like trying to find yourself when you don't know what route you want to go. Or having to make decisions that might hurt people that you really care about and having to deal with the guilt."

He thought about that. "You're not talking about obstacles, you're talking about decisions, and some obstacles may lead to decisions, but hurting others isn't part of the obstacle, it's part of the decision. You're confusing the two, I think. If you're leaving me, can you just *tell* me?"

Corinne laughed nervously and said, "Yes, Bobby, it's not

fair to you. I don't think we should be together anymore."

Bobby looked down and began to fidget with the fried noodles in the bamboo bowl. She saw the deep hurt in his eyes as she felt a terrible pain pass through her core. She was so hurt, but also felt a sense of relief at the same time.

"I think we should take a long break and maybe see other people. You might find it to be a good growing experience for yourself."

The waiter approached the table and said, "Phone fo' you. Girl crying. She said, 'Emergency.'"

Corrine hurried to the bar, where the barmaid was holding the receiver. She took it and heard a hysterical Eunice crying on the other end.

"...Honey, calm down. Calm *down*.... He did *what?*"

Corinne and Bobby rushed out of the restaurant and back to the station. As they pulled up, they saw her standing outside with a tall, very thin man who seemed frail in a Yankee cap, a black t-shirt, and jeans, and was smoking a cigarette that he held between his second and third fingers.

Corinne jumped out and ran to her. The man, she registered in passing, was at least seventy. She threw her arms around her sister and said, "What *happened?*"

"He—he wanted to stop in the bar and get a d-drink, so I said okay, but only one, because I didn't want Mom to smell it on my breath when I got home. So...so we got to the bar, and-"

"There's something not right about him," the man said. He was in here the other night too, and he was going on about his deceased wife, started doing shots and all, and we called him a cab and sent him home." He took a drag on the cigarette. "I think he's going off the deep end, and I am sorry that you got swept into it."

Corrine asked, "Where is he now?"

Eunice, wiping her nose and face said, "He took a few shots of Jack Daniels and then he started playing all sorts of loud and stupid songs on the juke box like the Sex Pistols and Pink Floyd. There was one point where he stood up on top of the tables and started singing to *The Wall*, really loud and obnoxious. I told him that he was being stupid and bothering everyone, but the more he drank, the more out of control he got, and then he..."

"He what?"

"He made a pass at me and I got nervous and backed away and he started yelling at me and getting really mean. Then. . .then he took my bag and ran out the door before I could reach him."

"He took your *bag*?"

"Yeah, and then I called you, because I didn't want to call the cops and get him in trouble."

The old man shook his head. "He ran up the steps to the train platform, but the train hasn't come since then."

Bobby ran up the steps with the girls behind him and

found Horace sitting on the bench. "Hey, man," Bobby said, "give Eunice back her bag, now."

The train had just appeared in the distance. Horace stood up and looked Bobby straight in the face. To Bobby it was as if the devil had consumed the man—he was a totally different person to the one he met earlier.

Horace screamed, "You want your fuckin bag? Here! Here's your fuckin bag." Moving in a slithery strut, he grabbed Corinne by the waist and licked her face. "You want some of this, huh? You *want* some of this?"

Bobby went to grab him, but before he could, Horace spun away from them. He spun so hard he lost his balance on the platforms edge and tumbled onto the tracks.

The train was coming on rapidly, and they all ran to the emergency phone, screaming for help, but it was too late.

HANGIN' TOUGH

MIKE CAPOSTO WAS PACING the hallway in the emergency room at St. Vincent's Hospital that Friday evening, shock and rage burning inside him. He was a grave young man who had moved up to detective by the age of thirty. Although serious in demeanor and a more responsible person than most people can be, he also possessed an unsurpassed compassion and fervor. Murray Bernstein, his partner and friend, was sitting in the hallway with his head in his hands, unable to console him.

They had become partners when Mike moved up to detective, and, like most cops, they were brothers first and cops second.

Murray was tall and blond, with emerald green eyes, and able to remain calm and communicate; Mike scared people into submission. The only responsibility Murray had aside from the force was his cat Minkle, of whom he had an eight-by-ten framed photograph of on his desk. Yet he and Mike worked smoothly together. He knew that Mike could be a hothead, but he himself was a voice of reason. Murray had a quirky, eccentric character, was married to the job, and utterly reliable; he hung his pants on clothes pins in front of his elevated bed so that he could slip right into them when he got called to a scene. This one had been a tip from a couple of old-school cops. All in all, Mike and Murray were a dynamic duo and always had one another's back.

Mary Deluca, Mike's wife, had been shot at the 120th Precinct, where they both worked, and no-one knew whether she'd make it through.

Mike continued to pace, and to approach the front desk. "Where's my *wife!*" he shouted at the nurse behind the counter, "and what are they going to *do* with her? I'm gonna fuckin' tell you something right now—if that perp didn't off himself, *I'm* gonna off him the fuckin' second I see him."

The nurse, whose nametag read *Mannino*, had long red nails, curly brown permed hair, and a short, pudgy physique, and she had for some time been getting less inclined to try to calm him down. Her big brown cow eyes widened when she spoke to him, and her mouth opened every time she felt the shock of his reactions, but her voice remained consistent and uninflected. "Mista Caposto, if you come up here and scream at me one more time, I'm gonna have to call security. Please sit yuhself down."

At that moment, Murray grabbed his shoulder, looked into his eyes, and whispered, "Enough. I know you're angry. Just try and sit down. You want somethin'? How bout some water or coffee?"

Mike let out a long breath and found a seat in one of the long corridors. But soon enough the panic in him again twisted into a stream of thought, and he began to cry. "She was standing there in that white dress at that altar, lookin' at me with those big blue eyes, and we were on that beach in the Keys making love in the middle of the night, and we were looking at those houses near Main Street." He kept thinking about the fifteen years of his life with Mary rushing through his mind.

Murray sat next to him like a solid protective wall, watching.

Mike was thin and had an olive complexion. About five-eight, he was likable but very serious, and the ability to remain professional and passionate while "on the job" was what bumped him up to detective. He'd thought long and hard about applying, he had taken the psych evaluation, and passed with flying colors. The day that he saw that he'd made Gold Shield on the precinct bulletin board, he'd stared at it for twenty seconds and then begun to scream Murray's name out loud.

Murray, in early that morning, had ambled out of the breakroom, looked at him, and said, "Welcome aboard, kiddo, welcome aboard."

Mike had grown up in an apartment complex in Oakwood Heights, Mary in a house in Port Richmond, but they'd met at Tottenville High School. The school was on the South Shore of Staten Island; Port Richmond was on the North. But she had relatives in Huguenot and asked to use their address to go to school there.

Her parents had pushed her to do it because she had a developmentally disabled younger brother named Johnnie who was going to be transferred to Tottenville High from the Hungerford School in the fall, and they'd wanted her to keep an eye on him. It was a feat when a Special Ed student matriculated into a mainstream high school. The Department of Ed had implemented a program to install pseudo Shop Rite Grocery Stores in certain schools, to provide students a skill set that they could use in the real world—stocking merchandise, working a cash register, bagging groceries. Johnnie had been accepted and was going to be working at the school's Shop Rite. The DeLuca family had been elated, and happy that Mary had found a way there, too.

It was where Mike and Mary became high school sweethearts. The first time he asked her out was during sophomore year. He nervously approached her while she was rummaging through a bag at the bottom of her locker and slamming books onto the middle shelf. "Ugh, I can never find it!" she muttered to herself, but stopped in her tracks when she stood up and found him standing very close to her. She flashed a big smile of relief at him and batted those eyes. They were in the same homeroom and would talk every morning. "Hi, Mike, how are you?"

"Can I help you find whatever it is you're looking for? And would you mind accompanying me to tonight's basketball game?"

She laughed nervously and stammered, "Yeah, um, *yeah*, that would be fun! . . . I have to visit Johnnie at the Shop Rite— wanna come with me?"

"I would be *honored* to take a walk with you."

They began dating after that, and by the time senior year rolled around they were elected the couple most likely to succeed.

During the spring months they went to the Great Kills harbor, where Mike's uncles and father housed their boats at the marina. They were serious fishermen, and Staten Island had the largest concentration of sea bass on the East Coast.

Mike loved to fish with them, and pictures all over his parents' wood-paneled living room attested to it. One year he even made it into the *Advance* because he caught the largest sea bass. The Caposto family was an institution. One of his uncles distributed some of the fish to local restaurants. Striped bass too, and flounder and clams, made their way through New York Bay to the Staten Island Kills. Mike reminisced with his grandpa about catching the clams in cages, cleaning them, and keeping the best batch for Grandma.

Mike and Mary used to make out on the beach near the large rocks set in the sand. Once the end of May hit, they knew they'd be sharing their space with the horseshoe crabs on their annual visit. Mike and Mary felt as if they were in their own little enclave of the world as they lay there and fell deeper in love. She would fall asleep with her eyes open, and for long minutes he'd get lost in her eyes, and when she didn't blink for more than thirty seconds, he knew that she had fallen asleep. At those moments, he'd tickle her feet and drive her crazy.

Mary worked at a pre-school then. She toyed with the idea of becoming a teacher before deciding to join the police academy. Sometimes she forgot to take the Crayola Chalk Sticks out of her backpack and had them with her on the beach.

While they spooned there, surrounded by rocks, she'd sing the lyrics to some of their favorite songs by freestyle artist Judy Torres. They had gone to see her in concert more than once and really liked her a lot.

She drew hearts on the rocks with the legend *Mike Loves Mary* or *Mike and Mary Forever*. He used to take those opportunities to lick her nose and ride his tongue from her nose down to her lip. She loved to nestle in his neck and give him love bites when he least expected it.

Mike was proud of himself for getting a pretty blonde with enough energy to run a small army. Mary DeLuca was his reason for being.

She had graduated from the Academy a couple of years back and worked Narcotics. He knew her dedication was going to be a valuable asset to the force. She was one tough cookie—and she was crazy about him, too. They had recently been married, at Saint Roch's on Port Richmond Avenue, by Father Richard. It was Mary's family parish, and they were looking to buy an old Victorian in Tottenville to settle down in and start a family. This was what they wanted and they were working hard to get it.

Yet in that hospital corridor, all of it was meaningless, and all Mike could feel was his heart in his stomach. His knees were shaking, his head down, staring at the cup of coffee that Murray had pressed into his hands.

The doctor found them there and sat down next to Mike. Mike turned his head with tears in his eyes and looked at him.

"It doesn't look too good, kid. It doesn't look too good."

Mike threw the cup across the room.

2.

Mike had a Motorola beeper provided to him by the Department; as a detective, he couldn't drive a police car and had been instead assigned a brand-new champagne colored 1992 Taurus. He and Mary were big fans of New Kids on the Block, and *Hangin' Tough* was playing on the radio. He turned up the volume. He needed to get to the corner of Caswell Avenue and Willowbrook Road as quickly as possible. His adrenaline was always up when he was called to a scene. If there was any kind of distraction that could get him from Point A to Point B without overthinking what he was about to see, he was on it like white on rice. As of right now, New Kids on the Block was fine.

He was doing sixty cutting through the light traffic on Victory Boulevard. It was late afternoon, the sun had set, and the purple-and-orange glow on the horizon looked like a late-'80s exercise video.

He hung a sharp left onto Willowbrook Road, a quaint residential street that resembled many others on the Island and saw an older man, white-haired, briskly walking home from the bus stop. He turned when he heard the car turn the corner. They made eye contact, and then he stopped in his tracks and followed Mike's car with his eyes.

Mike had been to the corner before, notorious for collisions; the city had been trying to mandate an all-way stop sign there for years. But it took a long time for the politicians to get on the same page when it came to Staten Island. It was the third time in two years Mike had been there, being forced to analyze who hit whom first.

He and Mary had taken a *College Now* political science class together in high school that covered public policy and where the Island fit into the rest of the city. Most of the time, they had learned, initiatives never came to fruition. One time she had gotten so bored that she ripped off a piece of her brown paper-bagged text book cover and wrote, *Mike and Mary are part of the "I Don't Care Club"*, and passed it to him. She'd known that would make him smile and foster his attention; when he got the note, he'd glanced at her and seen her smiling face and those eyes batting at him in anticipation. It had put a smile on his face, as she knew that it would.

There was already a mob scene of local residents when he pulled up. Matt Pettegolezo, a retired FBI agent who lived on Caswell Avenue, had already reached the scene. Mike knew him from community board meetings and mutual friends as a community type, a pillar of safety. He seemed invariably to be wearing outdoor dickie pants in khaki and the most boring pair of New Balances that one could find. His t-shirt had grass stains on it from trimming his lawn every day. His features were masculine and rigid, standard-issue Italian American—you could barely see passion in his facial expressions—but he had adapted to the American lifestyle in every other way.

Mike hustled over to the white van that had crashed into the stop sign pole, flashing his badge to the crowd that was already moving back, muttering different things. One tall, lanky woman, daintily holding her keys because she had just made her way home from the corner nail salon and her long, bright-pink nails were still drying, said to a middle-aged guy leaning on his red convertible, which was blasting Pink Floyd, "I saw the guy fly outta the car. I don't think he got back up yet, I can't see."

"Oh, my God," he said, "you're kidding me."

Mike found Pettegolezo. He recognized somebody else also when he bumped into a man holding a blonde baby and wearing a white Speedo bathing suit. For a second he could not place him, but then he remembered going undercover one night at Father Cappodano Boulevard in South Beach and checking out a scene where a lot of gay men went cruising.

Dressed in black, he'd made his way to the ferry terminal at St. George to catch the train. Murray was going to pick him up at the Grasmere station, and they'd scope out the area together. They were hunting for a suspect who had been hitting delicatessens and stealing money out of the register. The consensus on that case had been that he was meeting men at the cruise sight and threatening them for a ride to the bridge and a good lay. There had even been nights when he would threaten to kidnap their babies, because most of the guys who went had been married with children.

In that split second on Willowbrook Road, Mike stared at the frail and pointed nose of the man holding the blonde baby, remembering that he had been there that night. They'd tried to interview him, but he had been extremely anxious, had refused to disclose any information and kept his head down, a cigarette dangling from his mouth. He'd said he didn't remotely know what they were referring to.

As Mike past him, the recognition became mutual, but neither spoke. The man turned to his petite wife, who was standing behind him, and said, "Let's bring the baby in, honey."

Mike continued to the corner where the EMTs had been moving a very heavy man onto a stretcher. Pettegolezo turned to Mike, exasperated and unassuming, and said, "The guy in the white van hit the stop pole and got ejected. The other car fled the scene as soon as he could."

Mike was framing a few questions when his beeper went off. He glanced at the screen and saw *1013 SCREAM*, the order to report back to the precinct immediately because there was an *EMERGENCY*.

At that moment, the driver who had left the scene pulled around the corner in his 1974 boat of a Chevy, and all the neighbors started to shout, "That's *him*! *There's* the asshole!" The guy in the Chevy tried to flee the area again but pinned the woman with the pink nails onto the red convertible.

Mike was beside himself, but his beeper continued to go off.

Just then, Murray showed up at the scene from the other end of Willowbrook, slammed his vehicle to a stop, and leaped out of the door. "Mike!" he shouted. "Mike, you gotta get to the precinct. *Now!*"

Mike turned with his hand on his head. "Do you fuckin see what just *happened* here?"

Murray began to cry and, looking at Mike, said, "*Listen* to me! It's Mary, and it ain't good."

"Mary? What happened to Mary?"

"Perp shot her in the head, and they rushed her to the hospital."

Mike froze.

"Come on, man. You gotta be strong now, you gotta be strong and get over to the hospital *now.*"

3.

The doctor said he wanted Mike to speak to some of his friends at the police department and then guided him into the waiting area, where three cops were sitting. Mike didn't know what to say to them or do. They'd never seen him like that.

He sat down and began to sob profusely as Freddy Jones wrapped an arm around his shoulders and said, "The perp killed himself after he shot her. He's gone, Mike. Gone."

Mike looked up at him and nodded, for some odd reason

remembering the time the two of them had responded to a call from the senior center at Mariner's Harbor. An old woman had locked herself into the bathroom and was afraid to leave it. Jones had broken the lock to get in, and as he opened the door, muttered to Mike out of the corner of his mouth, "If she's naked, you're paying for the beer tonight."

Nurse Mannino called Dr. Thomas to the front desk and spoke softly to him. Then he turned to Mike and the others and said to him, "I'd like for you to come and see Mary now."

Mike rose and followed him to Room 115B. He was used to taking perp walks, but this was a different beast. He kept trying to not think about what he was about to see.

Then he heard Murray's voice in his head as if God had come down from the sky and given him strength: "You got to be strong Mike, you gotta be strong."

He entered the hospital room and saw her attached to machines and wires. He noticed that her eyes were open and appeared to be looking up at the ceiling. The doctor turned to him and told him that she had begun to have some rapid eye movement, which was a good sign in cases like this.

Mike looked at her, tears in his eyes, and then turned to the doctor and said,

"With all due respect, I'm sorry, but my wife sleeps with her eyes open. So I may have to raise my voice a little to see if she's responding."

The doctor looked at him and said, "I can tell that she's

responding sir, I don't think it is necessary too…"

At that instant Mike screamed, "Mary, *wake up!* Wake up *now!*"

Mary's eyes didn't move, they just kept looking up.

"Officer Caposto, will you lower your voice?"

Mike ignored the doctor. "Mary, it's time to *wake up!* Wake the fuck *up!*"

"I'm going to have to ask you to leave now," the doctor said.

Mary's eyelids fluttered.

"That's not *good* enough, Mary. That's not going to be *good* enough!"

Mary's head then turned towards him, "Mike, why are you yelling?"

"Because it's the only way I could get you to wake up."

"Do me a favor, just turn the radio up next time."

Mike laughed and squeezed her hand. "I knew you'd tough this one out."

DIARY OF A SCAPEGOAT

WAS STUCK IN SLEEP PARALYSIS, and my school skirt had ridden up like it did every afternoon when I got home, lay on my bed, and took a nap. My bed faced the door that everyone found necessary to open at any given moment. I was woken up by my grandmother, who was screaming that there had been a car accident outside in her loud, screechy Italian voice. "Ci fu un incidente d'auto al di fuori!" she cried repeatedly as she ran from her upstairs apartment to the living room, through the hallway, and to my bedroom door. You could have heard her on the other side of the world, but she persisted in thus repeating herself three times over. It began to make music in my head and sounded like the vocal stylings of Gigliola Cinquetti.

I couldn't see what was going on—my eyes were semi-open, and my room looked like cotton candy swirling in a machine, the blue walls and yellow rose border all meshed into one burst of pastel, and I couldn't quite get out of NREM.

I finally woke up and adjusted my school skirt. I had been rolling it up three or four times by then. My father had bought me a Sony MHC-BX3 mini hi-fi system. Daft Punk's new song "One More Time" was playing on the radio, and for whatever reason, it always put me in a good mood.

"Julia, Julia, *si sveglia?*" she asked me, and I crankily yelled,

"I *heard* you, Grandma." I got up and went outside. The city had failed to make any attempt to answer Staten Island's plea to turn the two-way stop sign on the corner of Caswell and Willowbrook into an all-way. There had been four accidents there already that year, and it was only September.

It was late afternoon, and it felt like you could touch the sunset from our house. Anytime this happened, all of our neighbors on the block, which seemed like the width and length of a large city pool, would make their way to the street. The crash was always loud, louder depending on the magnitude of the accident. For my grandmother, this brought excitement to a mundane and boring day. She took permanent residence on the terrace, what she called the "*terraza.*" Caswell Avenue was nothing like Brooklyn, and she'd never quite adapted to the quiet boredom that Staten Island had to offer. She was used to the Brooklyn way, and my mother was convinced that my grandfather had moved her here on purpose.

My neighbor Mr. Matt Pettegolezo, who was an FBI agent, had already made his way over to the accident scene. He had rigid, masculine features, and very Italian American—you could see passion in his facial expressions—but he had adapted to the American lifestyle in every other way. He was *Everyman* for me.

Once my grandmother and I got close enough to see the accident, I could tell from Matt's behavior with the cops that it was someone we knew. Marina, the Italian American woman who lived across the street, and who referred to my grandmother as "the Italian woman across the street," was standing idly, waiting for Mr. Pignati to make his way over with the news. Ms. Hang, the Korean owner of the nail salon on the corner, was also curious to find out what happened. My grandmother and I continued up the block until we reached Mr. Tucci, who was leaning on his Toyota convertible. He would blast Billy Joel and Pink Floyd from his car and then play records in his yard all summer. My father always complained that *Guidos* tended to like what was good twenty years after the band's significance in culture had evaporated, and then they had the nerve to become fanatic about it and subject everyone else to it as well. Mr. Tucci wasn't friendly, but ever since I was little he had always found a way to look me up and down without hesitation. I said, "Hi, Mr. Tucci. You know who got hit?"

"Hey, sweetie, it ain't nothin. It ended up being just a little fender bender. I think it was Marty's wife from across the street." At that moment my cell phone began to ring. It was Richie, he told me he was coming to pick me up around seven, and that I'd better be ready.

2.

We were lying in bed watching *Good Will Hunting* for the eighth time. Richie loved it because the underdog makes it in that movie. Richie's mom was ordering us food from Go-Go Souvlaki, and I was spending as much time as possible there again. He had the train line riding through his yard every half hour. It sounded like it was going a hundred miles an hour after stopping at Oakwood behind Monsignor Farrell High School.

All of our friends had one thing in common; we were all Catholic school kids, and we were all poor. I was a Catholic school girl who had anti-Christian artists for parents, and Richie's mom Liz was a devout Catholic who went to church every Sunday after her husband left her with two kids. We found some common ground because we all had to work after school and on weekends to make ends meet.

We used these opportunities in Richie's room with the

door closed to try and fool around. I said "try"; all of our friends who were couples were already doing it—Erin and Liam, Emily and Christopher, Danielle and Raymond, and some others of the more affluent ilk. But we had some trouble, mainly because I didn't want to let it in, and that bothered me, and everyone knew it. I soon learned that, if you were doing it to please some guy, odds were it was going to be really painful because your libido, your mind, and your heart were not in it. However, if you were going to make *love* to someone, the pain might be there initially and would probably fade after some good, wholesome sex.

The first time Richie and I took a stab at it was at the Victory Motor Inn on Willowbrook Road. Richie didn't drive yet, so we had Liam and Erin drop us off there one night. It was really cheesy and tacky-looking on the inside. It had this super stucco, glittery molding around the reception window, which had a wood sign on the right that listed all the prices. They had a four-hour stay for $60.00. Richie used to make decent money mowing lawns for Jimmy Castani on Lighthouse Hill. What he made in a day, I made it in a week working as a hostess at Perkins Family Restaurant on Forest Avenue. He willingly paid that evening. I promised him that we would try and have sex after the previous Christmas when he bought me an *I Love You Plate* necklace, the ugliest, gaudiest and most cheaply made piece of jewelry that one could own. When I later pawned it for forty-five dollars, the jeweler explained to me that it was because the diamonds were diamond chips. I was bummed about that transaction.

An emaciated-looking man behind the counter, smoking a cigarette, slipped us the key. We took the stairs to a room on the second floor. All the while, Richie was holding my hand as I trailed along behind him. I noticed that his palms were sweaty and that he was trying to act cool as a cucumber but was really worried about how he was going to perform. It was his first time too.

We entered the room, which was as ugly as the reception desk and just as glittery. It had a mirror on the ceiling and a half-assed hot tub in the bathroom that I would not have bathed in if my life depended on it. We sat on the bed and had our usual banter. He looked at me and said, "Julie, you're the hottest girl in the world. I do not know what I did to get you."

He had lost a hundred pounds the year before I met him. He was a fat kid and came from a fat family. When I first met him, he was working at the Getty Gas Station on the corner of Clark and Amboy Road. He said that was when he started to lose the weight, and that he worked hard from that point on to keep it off. Shortly after Richie started working there, a kid from New Dorp High School started, too. He was a little strange and a bit of a pyromaniac. He "accidentally" set fire to the station one night. It was all over the *Advance,* and the owner decided to not hire any attendants under eighteen after that. That was the end of Richie's career as a gas attendant.

So Richie had always been self-conscious about his weight and had trouble getting naked in front of me at first. I was kind of unhappy about that because I was attracted to his sensitivity and wanted him badly. He had a round face and brown puppy-dog eyes. He would look at me sometimes, and I would just melt away. I wanted to share this with him, or at least I thought I did. I never had any trouble getting naked in front of him. After going through puberty and watching prime-time television in the nineties, I just thought that it was a normal occurrence to jump into bed with your first "real" boyfriend. My only previous experiences had been some dry rubbing with a prior boyfriend and a gyno appointment that really did not go that well.

Anyway, I was determined to sleep with him, and I thought that night was going to be The Night.

Well, we both got naked and did our usual foreplay. He would make me lie down and feel me up, we would play a little doctor and nurse, and then I would start to get really hot and bothered when he got up to the part where he would feel my breasts. There was no initial fingering or penetration to my vagina prior before that night. We'd kept it cool until then.

He lay on top of me and began to thrust at me with his penis, except that his thruster wasn't penetrating and I was getting anxious. I did not know why it wouldn't go in, but it didn't, and we both became increasingly more bummed about the situation. The tension began to build, and the encounter became more disappointing, and then suddenly I laid down to close my eyes and I felt Richie sit down at the end of the bed. He let out a big sob. I did not why he was crying or what he was crying about, but his sobs became ominous to me. At that moment, I thought that he was going to break up with me.

Instead, he turned to me and said, "I feel like the biggest fuckin *loosah*. I was nevah good at *nuthin*, not *anythin'*. I wanted to have this, and I suck at it, too."

I felt so for bad for him, and I told him that what he was saying was not true at all. "You have so much going for you," I said as I looked at him perplexed and sad.

He struck me with another sob of complete grief. "No I don't. Stop lyin' to me. I know you're lyin to me."

It made me think about a story that I'd heard from some of my friends who'd come to Villa from St. Charles, South Shore kids like Richie. They said they had a monsignor working at St. Charles who used to fondle the altar boys until he got tried and acquitted. Jimmy was an altar boy at St. Charles and had a few problems that he was trying to mask besides being a poor inner fat kid. In that moment, I got so consumed by his misery that I did not know what to do besides revert to complete fear. All of a sudden a complete clarity came over me and I was like, "Fuck it, let's just do it and get it over with."

He started laughing hysterically and said that we had to get dressed because Liam and Erin were going to be there in ten minutes to pick us up.

When they came to get us, I thought that the devastation he had felt, which was entirely about him, would have prompted him to say nothing. But it didn't. He climbed into the car and was like an open book. Liam and Erin were trying to be discreet, but about three minutes into the car ride they could not help themselves, and Erin said humorously, "So how did it go?"

Richie snapped, "It sucked, and we didn't do it."

I gave him a dirty look and then caught myself saying that we would try again soon and started talking to Erin about our new Science teacher, Mr. Weir. He was twenty-four and had poor classroom management.

My parents lived right near the Victory Motor Inn, so they just took me home that night. It was disappointing and changed my relationship with Richie for good.

3.

Richie's mom called us into the living room when the *Go-Go Soulvaki* came. They had three dogs that barked every time we needed to go outside and smoke a cigarette. She gave us the food and asked how we were doing. I liked talking to her because she'd recently decided to go back to school, and I thought that to be brave for someone her age who had lived a life as hard as she had. I knew she liked me a lot. As we sat in the living room, Richie's sister, Anita, a Villa alum and now Wagner College student, came in and completely ignored the fact that I was there. She was hard and mean. She'd loved me at first, but some girl that I worked with at Perkins had decided to be an asshole and ruin my happy, formative life by telling Anita that I'd said bad things about her. It was humorous. She ended up acting like a total "b" to me from that point on, except for the time that we were at the Player's Place, our home bar, where she got drunk and proceeded to tell me that she didn't hate me, she just disliked anyone who hurt her baby brother.

I found *that* funny, because *I* was the one losing my mind all the time. I was either home crying in my bedroom, or I was crying somewhere in the lunch cafeteria. It didn't seem like Richie cared that much when he was hurting me, unless it was one of those blow-out fights that we ended up having, which would usually lead to us crying together. We were in love, and no one could deny that. But he needed to live the macho life and do the macho thing like all the other city-workers on Staten Island, and that's what he came from, a family of city-workers. While we were sitting in the living room, in order for Anita to make sure that I was having the most unpleasant time possible, she decided to ask Richie how his trip to Lipsticks with Rob Borio the night before had been. Rob Borio was the local drug dealer and was all of about twenty years old. He also had a black market side business selling fake IDs.

Richie went about fifty shades of red and said, "Anit, shut up and stop bein' a bitch."

She turned to him with her fat mouth full and dripping ranch dressing. "What? That's what youse said youse were gonna do."

Lipsticks was in a small local shopping plaza on Victory Boulevard. A lot of their new strippers were Russian girls who were new to the country and new to the easy amount of cash that they could make in one night stripping for the cops, firemen, and EMTs—especially the young guys, some of whom would blow their whole paycheck on one of these broads. The guys in the neighborhood would smoke some weed, blow a line, and could not wait to get their hands on one of these *chicas*. Danielle's older brother was involved with one and, from what I could infer, those Russian girls would take it one step further than most women in that line of work. They would start relationships with some of these city-workers because they had benefits. Coming from communist Russia, they wanted the benefits and the cash that came along with working that angle.

The subject got changed quickly when Uncle Larry came upstairs for dinner. He'd come to live with them when

Richie's dad left, and he was the only steady male influence that Richie had in his life. Every once in a while on a weekend night, he would let Richie use his Winnebago to take me out. We would indulge in some puff-puff passin' and other activities, if you get my drift. We would make it a point to pick up everyone we knew and hang out every once in a while. We would go to the deli on Amboy Road across the street from Angelo's Pizzeria. We would get a philly, a pack of Newport Lights, and a couple of snacks for after we got high. When it was nice out, we would park on the corner of Thomas and Woodbine and smoke in the "woods." I'll never forget the first night that we met the "guys," as my girlfriends and I use to call them.

4.

There were seven people in Danielle's family. We had just spent a long afternoon of anticipation in her room. It'd smelled like we'd taken a bath in Victoria's Secret's "Dream Angel." All of us were excited to hang out with the guys we had met at Danielle's house party the night before. They'd arrived just as the party was winding down. When they came in, we were passed out on Danielle's cream-colored, heavily embroidered couch, drunk on Ketel One and cranberry juice. I felt almost incoherent and really drowsy while lying there. It was similar to a couch that you would see at Levitz, a kind of imitation Victorian piece. While almost half asleep on one another, I could not help but observe that Danielle's arm was draped over her head and her long, neon-pink manicured nail was resting on her grandmother's "paint by the numbers" painting that hung above the couch. It looked like an imitation Thomas Kinkade, if one could believe that there was such a thing. It was actually somewhat pleasant to picture yourself in when looking at it. The painting had a stone path that created a depth of field leading to the focal point, a small stone cottage with lit windows in the middle of the woods. It had patches of grass on either side and was surrounded by trees. If you looked closely at it, you could see a city or village in the distance.

Danielle's grandmother was quite a trip. She gave me a ride home once and asked me whether or not I liked yellow people or brown people better. I was speechless and didn't know what to say, so she said that she liked yellow people better because they were lighter, but she prayed for everyone.

Erin, Emily, Danielle, and I were sitting on that one couch while Anna occupied the matching chair. After staring half asleep at Danielle's fingernail, I noticed that my head was spinning. I held it up and I felt a little better. I looked down and began to stare at the leopard sandals I had bought at Steve Madden. It somehow seemed as if they had begun to move on their own and become sea leopards in Danielle's seafoam-green carpet ocean. I felt whoever was sitting next to me move and then realized it was probably Emily, because she started to call my name. "Julie? Jules? Are you okay?"

I was swaying back and forth when she said that. I went to lift my head up without answering her and bumped into the white wax candle of three little angels that was sitting on the glass-centered mahogany coffee table. Emily started laughing, and that helped me see straight again. I arose only to see Anna's mocking smile. She was always happy to see me fail or make an idiot of myself.

"I thought Liam was cute," Erin said as she looked in the mirror to make sure that her eye make up wasn't smeared and that her hair was as straight as a pin. She hated that her ash brown hair was so curly and unmanageable. "Jules, did I ever tell you about when I got my period and my hair started to grow in curly? There was one point when half my hair was straight and half curly. My sister used to find it hysterical!"

"Yes, Erin, about ninety times!"

"Don't turn around!" Emily screamed.

Emily would iron my hair every weekend; as a matter of fact, she ironed everyone's hair every weekend. Her mother was a hairdresser, and she had an amazing knack for it. She loved doing it, too. She and her sisters had the thickest hair I had ever seen. Their iron was ready to combat any hair that came its way. "I would never do it for a living," she would say, "because I'm really afraid of other people's opinions, and my mom told me that's what the job is all about."

Emily was a creative person, but she was shy and apprehensive in many situations. Once she had me return her bra to Victoria's Secret because she was afraid the saleslady might question why she was returning it. I never hesitated to help Emily out because she was my Donna Martin from 90210. I loved her carefree attitude towards most things. It reassured me that my neurotic behavior was frivolous and unwarranted on a daily basis. I don't ever think that she knew how much I relied on her, but I needed her and I think that she needed me, too.

Anna walked in sporting her grey sweat pants and her new, bright green Gap fleece sweatshirt. "Hello, everyone. Hello, hello, hello!" she screeched in her high-pitched voice. She came into the bedroom, where she saw me sitting on the bed.

"Julie, why are you so dressed up?"

"I don't know," I said in a snappy tone.

She looked at me with an envious eye, as if I were sitting there in an evening gown. I was wearing a pair of slacks, a red tank top, and high-heeled vinyl boots.

"You are like way too dressed up to be hanging out on the corner of Thomas Street."

Anna and I never got along. Her family owned a pizzeria on the South Shore. She was first-generation Italian like me, but her family fit the stereotype much more than mine did. I never had a response to her smug remarks. I just walked out of the room feeling annoyed and insecure. Danielle lived in a large corner home on the corner of Thomas Street and McKinley Ave in Richmondtown. It was set up like a loft, the ceiling high enough to see up to the third floor. There was a hallway overlooking the entrance and living room.

As I went to use the bathroom, I looked over and saw Edna teeter in through the front door. I ran back into Danielle's room to warn her that her mother had gotten home from the Marina Café. It was Saturday night. Danielle told everyone to keep it down.

Edna had come home drunk again. It had been about two years now since Danielle's dad cheated on her mom and left, though he showed up every so often. He left Edna the mortgage, the family's Boar's Head route, and five kids. Edna made it up to the second floor, screaming at the top of her lungs, "You know why I do this? You know why I come home drunk every fuckin' weekend? Because your father *cheated* on me and left me here with five fuckin' *kids!* *That's* why!"

Danielle's door was closed, and we were all sitting there nervously as Danielle rocked back and forth on her bed with her hands over her ears. Her little sister Molly was down the hall, sitting on her bedroom floor watching TV, when Edna stumbled into her room. She began screaming again, "*Tell* me. Tell me *why?*"

"I don't *know,* Mom, I don't *know.*"

The next thing we heard was what sounded like a slap across Molly's face. Danielle began to sob right away. Edna's feet fell heavily into the hallway. She stumbled back to her room at the other end of the hall and slammed her door.

As soon as Danielle heard her mother's bedroom door close, she quietly opened hers. This was a common occurrence in Danielle's house, and she knew that, if her mother heard her going to her sister's rescue, things would only get worse.

Just as Danielle was about to leave her room, she turned around, eyes on the floor, and asked if anyone would go with her. She felt her mother would calm down if she left her room and saw her with someone else. Everyone sat there awkwardly. We were all waiting for Erin to say yes, because she was Danielle's best friend. She would have been the best candidate, because Edna loved Erin, had even taken her in on several occasions. After a few more seconds of silence and staring at one another, I volunteered to go. I didn't say anything, just got up and walked to the door. Nicole looked at me with tears of embarrassment.

As we made our way down the hallway to her sister's room, Danielle wouldn't look at me. I noticed that the Mac eyeliner had run down her face. We'd each bought a stick together a week before at the mall.

Molly's head was under the pillow when we entered. We heard a muffled sob. You could tell from her breath she was trying to stop crying. I stayed at the door as Nicole touched her shoulder. The girl's head was still under the pillow.

"Please, no, don't—"

Danielle whispered in her ear, "It's me, not Mommy."

Molly removed the pillow from her face, which was now beet red. She had been watching *The Price is Right*. Bob Barker's blonde beauties were sitting on a Jacuzzi that one of the contestants had just won. She had it on mute.

Molly and Danielle kept staring at each other and crying. She had sat up by then and noticed that I was standing at the door. She smiled at me. Molly had a friendly disposition and a good attitude.

As I was about to sit on the end of the bed, we heard Edna's door swing open, and I froze. Danielle and I turned to each other. Edna was screaming again, "And you know what *else*?"

She wobbled into the room, having changed into her race-car t-shirt and black stretch pants. She caught herself when she saw me and stopped in her tracks for a second. She looked at me.

"Look who it is—the skinny bitch, the little, skinny, quiet bitch that comes here and cries all the time. Wah-wah! Are you still crying over your ex-boyfriend, honey? I stayed twenty years and had five kids with my sonofabitch ex, and you know who he's with now? Some *whoowah*, some fuckin' *whoowah*! How do you like that?"

She came closer to us; she must have just brushed her teeth, because I could smell the Colgate and gin on her breath while she puffed on her Merit cigarette. She grabbed Danielle's ear. Danielle closed her eyes in shame and Edna bent down to her and snarled, "Don't come home late tonight *or else!*"

She stomped out of the room and into her bedroom, slamming the door repeatedly like a child. She screamed again, "You hear what I said, Danielle? Did you fuckin' *hear* it?" Danielle sat there, trying to light one of her sister's Newport Lights with a match. She accidentally burnt her newly painted, bright pink plastic nail and muttered, "Shit! . . . *Yes!*"

When we went to meet the guys that night, we thought we'd be friends for life.

5.

The funny thing about attending Saint John Villa Academy for Girls is that it was a good Christian school with good Christian values. Their motto was "We are building, not only strong women of character, but a world where the Kingdom of God is truly alive." Except for when it came to collecting money from their students and supporting families. We were sitting in homeroom, which took place in the cafeteria every morning. They had us separated in alphabetical order with our fellow classmates for the appropriate year. I was in the P–Q section. It was the third semester of our junior year, and report card distribution day. My homeroom teacher for that year was Mrs. Stravinsky—in her early thirties, pregnant, and uber nerdy, she had an annoying lisp and greatly disliked me. She smelled like she dropped on a little bit too much of Clinique Happy that morning. I knew that's what she was wearing because she used to buy it every few months from my aunt at the Macy's counter in the Staten Island Mall. The content area that she taught was Physics. I didn't get to take Physics because my parents were paying $5,000 a year for me to be in a standard program in which I didn't graduate with a Regents diploma.

My girlfriend Angela De Marco, who was in Honors, used to imitate her: "Girls, Physics is everything. Physics is life. When the sperm hits the egg, that's Physics." I asked her if Physics had to do with the fact that I hadn't received my report card that day. She grimaced at me and had no answer except to tell me to ask Sister Ann, our principal. Sister Ann was a phony woman. She spoke softly, looked at all the girls up and down as they passed her by, and smiled lovingly— unless she was screaming at you because you hadn't brushed your hair or your skirt was rolled up too high. There were also times when she became short and cross out of nowhere. I'll never forget the year that I joined Glee Club and my parents came to see me perform. My father accidentally dropped the plastic forks that they provided for the minimal serving of pastry they gave you. Sister Ann couldn't help herself and curtly exclaimed, "Well, now you can pick them all up." She quickly apologized, kindly said that she would send someone out to buy some new ones.

That wasn't my last encounter with her. Anna and I got caught smoking cigarettes in front of Hooters on Hylan Boulevard. Sister Ann pulled up in her silver Infiniti and demanded that we see her as soon as we got to school the next morning. We avoided it, but it didn't avoid us. We got into a lot of trouble and had to see Klep, the gym teacher turned dean. She could not believe that we were sitting in her office. She was like, "Did you two ever get detention before? You are so off the radar usually." It was a weird disciplinary act. It was like calling us prudish and uncool while punishing us for smoking cigarettes in uniform. They didn't care that you were killing yourself with cigarette smoke; they only cared that you were doing it in uniform.

So I didn't know what to expect when Mrs. Stavinsky suggested that I go and see Sister Ann. My grades had dropped considerably since I started dating Richie. I felt that I was in a lot of trouble. On my way out of the cafeteria and to my first period class in the annex, I saw Danielle walking by herself. She looked down, and I was curious why, so I approached her. She had been crying and broke down about how she hadn't gotten her report card. I told her that I hadn't either, and she asked me if I knew why. "No," I said. "I'm trying to not go and see Sister Ann."

She looked at me sadly, with tears lining her bottom eyelids and her lip trembling, and said, "It's because we didn't pay tuition."

I was stunned, hurt, and humiliated all at the same time. Danielle mentioned that her mom was coming that day to talk to Sister Ann. She asked me if I wanted to sneak to her car and smoke a cigarette during third period. I said that I would meet her on the corner of McClean and Father Cappadano Boulevard.

When I did, she was already on her second cigarette. She had just bought a new pack at the corner deli. Ugh, how I hated recess-filtered Parliaments. But beggars cannot be choosers, and god knows Danielle gave me plenty of cigarettes.

We talked about our encounters that morning. She said that Mr. Burke had at least been nice enough to pull some of the girls who hadn't received their report cards over to the side. He was just as frustrating as the rest of the teachers, but at least he was able to make you laugh. I also think that, deep down, he was a kind and gentle person. Most of the girls thought that he was gay and asked him about it once. He turned several shades of red and said that he did not feel comfortable answering that question. Once Erin said that she saw a picture of a pretty lady in his wallet. However, I had taken him every year for theology and life and death and he'd never mentioned a woman in his life.

I didn't go to see Sister Ann that day. I was obviously down and out. My old best friend, Tara Rossini, the reason why I was going to that stupid school in the first place, asked me why I was so upset and said that I could confide in her. I didn't want to because I felt betrayed by her, too. But she owed me for saving her when she fainted. I guess she felt bad. We had been sitting in Sociology a few weeks earlier, and Ms. Donner had been telling us in her deep voice about a case study done by a sociologist on a feral child. She intricately explained the ins and outs of this poor and unfortunate child's horrific story. Her father had wrapped her up in a crib for thirteen years and never let her see the outside world. He would only unravel her to use the bathroom. It ended up that he was a PTSD veteran and sat at the window with a gun all day as well.

After a few more minutes of the residual effects of this girl's case, Tara Rossini fainted right in front of me. I called her name several times and then ran from the annex building to the school nurse in the main building. I got the ambulance there as soon as possible. Oddly, we were both daughters of Vietnam veterans ourselves, born in the Eighties. I wondered if that had anything to do with her fainting. Who knows? We had known each other since we were five, and it happened that her mother was a recluse. But they thought of my family as demonic people because they let me go out and trusted me to make smart decisions.

Needless to say, our friendship ended early in our high school career. The worst decisions my parents made were having me hang out with Tara Rossini and her ignorant family. There were times that I went there when her mother would have me sit and watch them eat dinner because my father was late picking me up.

Anyway, I wasn't about to confide in Tara about not being able to pay my tuition. It was like something out of that *Welcome to the Dollhouse* movie, except it was a lot easier for me to escape, because she wasn't my mother. I went home that day, took a long afternoon nap, and wanted at all costs to avoid having a discussion with my mother. A few years earlier my parents had lost their silk screening studio in Manhattan, in which my father used to do high-end commercial work. We all suffered, especially my brother. He had to stop attending NYU because we could no longer pay for it, and it had been my father's dream to have him go there. It was where he'd wanted to go once he got out of Vietnam, but the government had denied the loan, and he'd worked hard to mold my brother into a fine young artist, only to watch it go down the tubes. It was safe to assume that delinquent tuition would be a touchy subject.

We lived in Westerleigh, which none of my friends understood because they'd all grown up on the railroad line. Staten Island's working transit line went straight from St. George to Tottenville. Danielle's little sister said to me once that she did not understand where I lived because there was no train. If you grew up on the North Shore of Staten Island

and attended a Catholic high school, odds were you went to Moore Catholic. That's what my brother had done, and that's what I should have done. Our home in Westerleigh was a two-family. My grandparents had lived upstairs until my grandfather decided to go food shopping one day and never came back. We found out a year later that he was living with a woman named Rhoda in a trailer in Clearwater, Florida. He never lived with us permanently again.

My mother finally came home. I'd just come out of the bathroom, which was directly across from the side door that we used as an entrance. My mother hated our house, hated that she'd lived with her parents her whole life, and hated that she had to commute into Manhattan for work every day. She'd worked for KWA Airlines since she was eighteen years old and thought that my father's business would eventually free her of that misery. She didn't usually come home in the happiest mood.

She was one of the prettiest women I had ever known. She was about five foot seven and had pale skin that looked like it should have freckles, but didn't. She was slender and trim, her eyes green, her face angular and sensitive. We only paid taxes on airline tickets, and we traveled quite often. She'd also worked across the street from Saks Fifth Avenue for about thirty years, which made retail therapy hard to resist.

I was at a standstill and didn't want to bombard her with

the news right away. My father had been home since about five o'clock from his school picture-taking job. I never spoke to him about money matters because he didn't handle the finances. Plus when I woke up from my long afternoon nap, he was screaming on the phone at one his sisters in Long Island. That was how he communicated with them. I had come to learn that they didn't *know* how to speak to one another, they just screamed. My father's family was in the middle of legal battle over their family estate that my father was losing badly. He was trying to keep his family together, and they wanted nothing to do with him. I was not going to communicate with him about tuition.

I came out of the bathroom and looked straight across to my mother standing there; she looked at me and asked, "What's wrong?"

I blurted in a frustrated tone, "I didn't get my report card today because you didn't pay tuition."

She knew she was late, but it was a tight month because she'd given me money for my junior prom limo, my high school ring, and bought me my junior prom dress—the things my classmates and I valued at Saint John Villa Academy for Girls.

She looked hurt, though, and seemed disappointed in herself. She absolutely hated that we were in that circumstance. After she put her pocket book down in the kitchen and I sat at the table, she looked at me and asked me if I had told my father. I didn't have to answer because he was still screaming into the phone at his sister, in Sicilian no less, *"Le non e' migliore di te,"* which means, "She's no better than you." My father always tried to make my aunt Melcora feel less inferior because she would continue to get screwed by my aunt Dina on several occasions.

We recently found out that my cousin Madalegna was a super success because she'd married a very wealthy man who owned two hundred-year-old restaurants in Long Island and was about to own a third. Apparently he had bought her some sort of Great Gatsby Estate in Manhasset with seven bathrooms. This type of stuff his sister would call and tell him about sent him into screaming frenzies that usually ended with him hanging up on her. Then you would know that he was going to be in the most delightful mood. My mother sullenly went into the living room and sat down, unwillingly ready to listen to the report he was about to make about his conversation with Aunt Melcora. "You know what stupid just told me?"

My mother replied, "I don't give a shit because we can't pay your daughter's tuition."

"...How come?" She told him because we were short on money that month. She also brought to my attention that Theresa Russo's mother had not yet cashed the check for the limo. I knew that was some sort of scam to begin with, because Theresa Russo's father was a hitman for John Gotti.

He had been in jail for a little over a year by then, and the mother had forced us to pay her even before she booked the limo. Theresa and I had developed a relationship that was semi-friendly. We would go to the mall and things like that. She'd come by and pick me up in her Honda Accord, and my neighbor, Mr. Pettegolezzo, must have noticed. He was the FBI agent who'd cracked the Gotti case. He told my dad that I shouldn't mention that he lived next door to me, because, if she knew, Theresa's mother might not allow her to hang out with me anymore.

Shouldn't it have been the other way around? From what Pettegolezzo told my dad, it was news to me that she had been trained to immediately hide the jewelry in the vault when the cops came to the house, which happened more frequently than it should have.

My mother determined to call my grandfather in Clearwater and asked him for the money. He had sent me a thousand dollars for my sweet sixteen, but she'd used it to help pay for the party.

The next Saturday morning, we were sitting in the living room. Our white wireless phone was resting on the mahogany end table next to our off-white couch. She picked up the phone and began to dial Grandfather's phone number in her packed-to-the-brim phone book, in which all the information was written out so neatly in her handwriting, in capital letters. I was surprised that she hadn't yet imported all those numbers into an Excel sheet, since that was her specialty at work.

There was a stained glass kaleidoscope next to the phone. I was so nervous about how the call would turn out that I froze and began to zone out on the colors in the scope. By the time I was done, the call was over. He was going to mail the check that day.

Mom was always sad after she spoke to him. I never knew him well because I had only been seven when he left. I was sad that this was happening, and I didn't know what to do.

The next morning I came in and had my usual morning breakfast with Anna. We had a free first-period class together, and the cafeteria at that time was fairly empty. The lunch lady, Annette, was a delightful and charming character. Her lip liner, eyeliner, and maybe even her lipstick were tattooed onto her face. It seemed to me that she was trying to achieve a look that resembled Elvira, Mistress of the Dark. When I was a child, Elvira had always scared me. I'd had a nightmare once that she was one of my grandfather's mistresses, and that, as I went upstairs to see my grandma, I found her there instead, sitting in black light with her legs crossed.

Anna and I got the usual. It depended on who got there first, who was usually the person to order: two French vanilla coffees and two buttered rolls. Sometimes the rolls were stale. It depended on what day of the week it was. But they always seemed to have what Annette liked to call *mootzies*. That was the most bastardized pronunciation for mozzarella sticks that I ever heard in my life. It was quite amusing. Anna and I never wanted mozzarella sticks at 8:30 a.m. We always passed. Anna had just started driving, and her Dad had bought her a Civic, so that there were five cars in her family. I'm sure that it was a tax write-off for the pizzeria. My family had one old and little beat-up car, a black 1995 Toyota Corolla. The new Civic was the typical car a Staten Island girl drove. It was the one thing that she had on me. She and I had always had a bitter and resentful relationship. She liked Richie, and he liked me. We ended up dating and decided to break the news to her one night on Danielle's front porch. It was awkward for all of us, but we left amicably.

So we had breakfast together every morning. Though I had taken Driver's Ed early that year, I ended up getting into four car accidents with my friends before my sixteenth birthday. One of them consisted of Vanessa Onesto and me on the corner of North Gannon and Bradley Avenue. There were four other vehicles in her father's car by the time the accident happened. We remained unscathed. Vanessa was from the richer side of town. Her father was an attorney who had his own law firm in Manhattan and a mild habit of sleeping with his Sri Lankan secretaries. They had a huge house in Annadale, where my father's childhood friend had built and contracted some very expensive McMansions. The South Shore of Staten Island, which was nothing but farmland and wide-open spaces until 1964, when the bridge was built, had become what I liked to call Guido Nation.

Anna and I got to talking, and she asked me how everything was going. It had become national news that I hadn't yet received my report card. The entire conversation veered in that direction, and I had no room to work my way out of it. I immediately began to feel my face tense up when she mentioned that she had received a "D" in English. She looked at me with her big cow eyes and her sarcastic tongue and said, "What did you get?"

I began to twitch, opening and closing my eyes repeatedly and trying to relax the crease in my forehead with my hand. I looked at her and said, "I don't remember."

I chugged my French Vanilla and told her that I forgot I had to meet Mr. Burke before second period to discuss my project for Life and Death.

"Oh, yeah," she said. "I totally forgot you had to do that." I told her that I would catch her later and sat in the bathroom for fifteen minutes.

On my way out, I saw Emily, my saving grace. She was always a breath of fresh air. We had Ms. Messina's English class together. I had been placed into standard when I was a Freshman and asked to move up to honors, but I'd never wanted to take the summer classes necessary to achieve that status. Emily had been placed in honors off the bat but had been demoted to standard because she did not have the grades to sustain honors status. So there we were, first generation Italians sharing the common bond of not graduating with a Regents diploma. I often wondered why it was so easy to live in the moment when I was in high school. That was probably because I never wanted to think about my bleak academic future.

Emily and I walked past the library doors at the end of the corridor and through the double doors that led to where our English class was being held. We stopped abruptly in the hallway when we heard Edna Affari's loud, smoke-ridden laugh. It was deep and shook me right to my bone. We glanced at her, looked at one another, rolled our eyes, and discreetly made our way into the classroom. Luckily Ms. Messina wasn't sitting there, because she and her husband used to be regulars at Perkins, where I worked. She was almost as loud as Edna Affari and always brought up that she'd seen me there. I'd received the English award from her for the past two years, and when my parents were unable to take me to the award ceremony, she would offer to come and pick me up. I thought that was sweet.

We sat in the back corner of the room, near the windows, and made sure we had enough paper to pass notes during class. Danielle passed our classroom on her way to Chemistry lab and stopped in, looking really happy. As I looked up, I saw her quickly running towards the back of the room. She had a smile on from ear to ear.

"What's up?"

She whispered in my ear, "My mom just paid the nuns off by bartering cold cuts for the convent in lieu of my tuition!"

While I sat there and processed that, I looked up at Danielle, sincerely trying to share in her joy. But my smile was so phony I could feel it. I didn't know how to respond, except of course by letting out my angst through writing Emily a series of angry letters full of malaise and anxiety.

6.

As I stood on line, waiting to use the payphone in the dreary school cafeteria, I fidgeted with the *I love you* plate that Richie had bought me for Christmas. It weighed about ten ounces. The legend was written in script made out of diamond chips and placed on a fourteen-karat gold plate. He kept telling me that he'd spent a total of four hundred and fifty dollars on it at L'Amore Jewelers in the Staten Island Mall. You could tell it was worth about forty-five dollars, though, and that whoever had sold it to him saw him coming a mile away.

"Richie. Richie! Do you *hear* me?" I screamed through the crappy pay phone in the corner of the cafeteria. I was leaning up against the set of two-by-four-inch beige boxes that they called lockers. Every day there was a line of girls at lunch just waiting to use the pay phones to speak to their boyfriends. Richie had bought me a beeper so I could beep him when I was about to call him.

"Liam just fuckin' knocked the glass out of the bottom of the door on the fourth floor. The ambulance just came to get him," he said, breathless but excited.

"What? Why the hell did he do that?" I was trying not to look too surprised, as Mr. Burke sat across the room staring at the line of girls lined up to speak to their more than likely future husbands. He had spoken of his disappointment about this matter several times. We were supposed to be America's bright young female future, yet the only thing that was ever on our minds was what our boyfriends were doing and making sure that they were with us and only us.

Mr. Burke had taught in many all-girls' facilities in the Staten Island–Brooklyn area and had a good sense of humor. Any time we didn't understand something, he would call us "Helen." It was an allusion to Helen Keller. Anyway, he would tell us stories about these girls who would jump off buildings and kill themselves because some Guido shmuck would leave them for some better-looking Guidette. Most of those stories took place in the Sixties with first-generation Italians, although, if you looked around the room, the situation hadn't changed much. We all had *I love you* plates and promise rings, and didn't really care about anything else but our boyfriends.

"Fuckin', fuckin' Father Phil caught him in the bathroom smokin' again. He just finished thirteen detentions for getting' caught a month ago. The rule is if you get caught again' then you gotta serve suspension' and that would look real bad to his navy recruiter. God only fuckin' knows what he's gotta serve now."

"Oh my god, is he okay?" I asked, truly concerned for his well-being. Liam was the only one of our guy friends who ever really acted like a man. He lived in the Tyson apartment projects on Tysens Lane. He was poor, living in project housing, and going to Monsignor Farrell High School for Boys. That had to give you a shitload of insecurities that you didn't need. His dad had died when he was four, and his mom was a secretary. His only ticket out of here was a ticket to the navy. It was a really big thing for Erin, because she didn't want him to go; she really loved him, and he really loved her.

"I gotta go. I gotta go find Erin. She's in class right now," I said in a frenzy.

"Don't be tellin' Erin too much—we don't know nuthin' yet," he said in a condescending, misogynistic tone.

"Okay, okay. I gotta go."

I looked at Anna and Emily, who were patiently waiting on the long lunch line. "We got *mootzies*, frenchies, and rollups," shouted Elvira's doppelgänger.

I approached them and said, "We have to go find Erin. Liam got hurt at school today, and the ambulance came to get him. I think he hurt his leg bad."

Emily and Anna's already big eyes had popped out of their heads, and they looked really worried.

When we found Erin, she could tell from the looks on our faces that something was up, and she began to blush. "What's the matta? What's the matta, Julie?" she asked in hurried, frightened anguish.

I said, "Liam got hurt at school today because he got caught by Father Phil smokin' in the bathroom again. All I know is that he was pissed off and kicked the glass out on one of the exit doors at school. He hurt his ankle."

She stood there as white as a ghost and began to cry.

7.

I had my father drop me off at Richie's that night; it always got awkward because he'd stopped showing his face around my house. I was angry about that, but what could I say? I loved him, and I didn't want anyone else to have him.

I went into Jimmy's house, where his mother and sister were sitting, watching *Whose Line Is It, Anyway*, and his mom, always happy to see me, looked at me and immediately asked how Liam was and what was going on with that whole thing. She was heavy but had a really sweet face, and I could tell from her wide-eyed look and expression that her concern was sincere. She knew how much Richie and Liam cared for one another and also knew that Richie might have stayed out of trouble when Liam was around. I said, "I haven't heard anything, but we're going to see him tonight, and I think that we'll get a better idea of how things went at the hospital today when we get to his apartment."

Liam hadn't known that he lived in a New York City housing project until one day, when Christopher's mom was dropping him off, she mentioned that she didn't know that she could "get to these projects taking Ebbits Lane." Mark seemed unaffected by that comment, because he'd only heard one of the old timers from the building call it that once. Some kidnappings and brutal murders had taken place there. I knew of a story from about twenty years before that spoke of a little girl named Andrea who had been kidnapped and never found. They claim that Rand had committed it along with several other crimes, but there was also talk of there being a level of satanic cult activity that went on somewhere in the woods. The woods were where we were headed once we picked everyone up and went to see how Mark was doing.

Richie and Liam worked up on Lighthouse Hill; they were always going on about the rich people's lawns that they use to mow. Unaware of my background at the time, I thought the people who lived up on Lighthouse Hill had it made. I wanted it so bad—the professionalism, the nice house, the two cars, and even the dogs. Mark and Jimmy would tell us stories all the time about the psychologist who made them frozen moccachinos in the morning when they trimmed her bushes and the baker's house they used to work that resembled a gingerbread house. Nights when we didn't go to the buffalo trails, we sometimes smoked up on the hill, when we knew the cops weren't going to be out—when they'd just reached their quotas after handing out tickets left and right for a week. Then things would quiet down and we could dome out the van.

We took the elevator up to the fourth floor where Liam lived. His mom was sitting on the couch. They were intelligent people, and you could tell from Liam's gentlemanly behavior that he had been raised right. While we were walking through the hall and staring at the brown metal doors that made the hallway look like an institution or a hospital, Richie told me a secret. He looked at me with those cross, manly eyes that were sensitive and serious at the same time. Our friends had a habit of repeating things and recycling information that somehow got distorted. However, I knew, when Richie was telling me something that was not to be repeated, it turned me on a little bit. He said that Liam's recruiter had come by the week before, and that Liam had had to pull out his father's death certificate. He had gone to the store and bought a six pack of Rolling Rock right after, and he drank it by himself. Jimmy said that drinking by oneself meant that things were bad, really bad, and that he was not himself for that whole week.

I told that to Emily the next day, even though he told me

not to.

Richie found out about it and said to me on the phone the next day, "You are killin' me, Julie, you're *killin'* me, and I can't take it. I cried in the guidance office the other day because of you."

I sat there with my arms wrapped around my body and my head down, unable to think and only able to feel. Whenever I thought about our relationship, I began to buy into the fact that it was a lie and that I did not want to rationalize how toxic it had become. So I thought that just feeling at every moment of every argument would keep us going, and let me tell you, it did.

ABOUT THE AUTHOR

Kristin Pitanza is an adjunct lecturer at the College of Staten Island and Saint John's University, in which she teaches writing and education. She is a native Staten Islander and likes writing about her hometown. She also takes a large interest in adolescent development and literacy, helping students develop writing skills through the scaffolding of grammar to written text. She has helped develop department-wide curricula for her writing courses at the college. She has a M.A. from the Teachers College at Columbia University and is completing her doctorate at St. John's University.